The Widowmaker Unleashed

like creatures that lived near the men. They

RETURN OF THE LEGEND

"Do you know who you're talking to, old man?"

"Yeah. I'm talking to a bunch of drug runners who are about to leave the planet."

"We're not here after you. Let us pass."

"Not a chance."

"You got a death wish?" demanded the man. "Look around you. There are fourteen of us."

"That's okay," said Nighthawk. "We've got a big graveyard."

The man looked at him unbelievingly. "Who the hell *are* you, old man?"

"I've had a lot of names," answered Nighthawk. "The one that stuck is the Widowmaker."

The Widowmaker Unleashed

• ◆ • ◆ • ◆ • ◆ •

Volume Three of the Widowmaker Trilogy

MIKE RESNICK

BANTAM
SPECTRA ™

BANTAM BOOKS
New York Toronto London Sydney Auckland

THE WIDOWMAKER UNLEASHED

A Bantam Spectra Book / September 1998

SPECTRA and the portrayal of a boxed "s" are trademarks of Bantam
Books, a division of Bantam Doubleday Dell Publishing Group, Inc.
All rights reserved.
Copyright © 1998 by Mike Resnick.
Cover art copyright © 1998 by Donato Giancola.

ISBN 0-553-57162-1
Published simultaneously in the United States and Canada

Bantam Books are published by Bantam Books, a division of Bantam
Doubleday Dell Publishing Group, Inc. Its trademark, consisting
of the words "Bantam Books" and the portrayal of a rooster, is
Registered in U.S. Patent and Trademark Office and in other
countries. Marca Registrada. Bantam Books, 1540 Broadway,
New York, New York 10036.

PRINTED IN THE UNITED STATES OF AMERICA

WCD   0   9   8   7   6   5   4   3   2   1

To Carol,
as always

◆ ◆ ◆

And to Ed Elbert:
friend,
producer,
keeper of promises

Chapter 1

◆ ◆ ◆ ◆ ◆ ◆ ◆

The emaciated figure, its flesh hideously disfigured by the ravages of a virulent skin disease, lay perfectly still. Patches of shining white cheekbone protruded through the flesh of the face, knuckles pierced the skin of the hands, and even where the skin remained intact it looked like there was some malignancy crawling across it and discoloring it.

Suddenly a finger twitched. An eyelid flickered. The breathing, though weak, became more regular, and finally Jefferson Nighthawk opened his eyes.

"I'm starving!" he croaked.

"Of course you are," said the man in the white outfit. "You haven't eaten in more than a century."

"Am I cured, or did I just run out of money again?"

The man in white smiled. "You're not cured yet," he said. "I just brought you out of the deep freeze. But we finally *can* cure you, and we will in the coming weeks."

Nighthawk closed his eyes and sighed deeply. "Thank God!"

The man looked amused. "I thought the Widowmaker didn't believe in God."

"I believe in anyone or anything that keeps me alive," rasped Nighthawk.

The man in white leaned over him. "Do you remember my name?" he asked.

"Gilbert something."

"Gilbert Egan. I'm your physician. Or, to be more accurate, I've been your most recent attending physician while you were cryogenically frozen. In the coming days, you'll be in the hands of specialists."

"Help me up," said Nighthawk, reaching a hand weakly in Egan's direction.

"That wouldn't be a good idea, Mr. Nighthawk," said Egan. "Your body is riddled with eplasia, and you haven't used your muscles in . . . let me see . . . a hundred and twelve years."

"So it's 5106?"

"5106 Galactic Era," Egan confirmed.

"And my clone's been out there for five years?"

"Actually, your first clone died a few months after they created him."

"My *first* clone?"

Egan nodded. "They created a second clone two years later."

"I don't remember."

"I wouldn't allow them to wake you for that one. You were too weak. I felt we could only revive you one more time. This is it."

"This second clone—did he die, too?"

"Nobody knows. I have a feeling he's still alive somewhere out on the Rim, probably with a new name and a new face." Egan paused. "But he accomplished his purpose. He sent back enough money to keep you alive until the cure for your disease was discovered."

"I'll thank him when I see him."

Egan smiled and shook his head. "People have been looking for him for three years. You'll never find him."

"If I need to find him, I will," replied Nighthawk with certainty. Suddenly his body went limp. "What's the matter?" he asked, puzzled. "I've been awake for maybe two minutes and I'm exhausted."

"As I said, except for one five-minute interlude a few years ago, you've been in deep freeze for more than a century. All of your muscles have atrophied. Once we get you healthy again, you've got a lot of work to do with the physical therapist."

"Why am I so damned hungry?"

"All we did was slow your metabolism down to a crawl. We didn't stop it, or you'd have died. And no matter how slow it was, eventually you digested everything in your stomach. From time to time—actually, about every sixth year—we've fed you intravenously to keep you alive . . . but there's a difference between being alive and not being hungry."

"So can I get something to eat?"

"Not for a few days. We have to be sure your digestive system is functioning properly. A meal right now could kill you. As soon as you're moved to the hospital, we'll inject some proteins and carbohydrates directly into your bloodstream, enough to keep you going for a couple of days."

"Then what?"

"The doctors perform their magic and eradicate all traces of eplasia from your system—and then, since you still look like something from a child's worst nightmare, you'll undergo a month or more of reconstructive cosmetic surgery."

"How soon before I'm out of here and on my own?"

Egan shrugged. "That's up to you—two months, four months, a year, whatever it takes."

Nighthawk was silent for a moment. Then he

spoke again: "There was another man last time you woke me."

"Yes," answered Egan. "Marcus Dinnisen. Your attorney."

"Where is he now?"

"Who knows?"

"*I* want to know. His firm is in charge of my money."

"Not anymore. Your second clone sent five million credits back with Ito Kinoshita and instructed him to pay it directly to us as we required it, rather than to allow the money to pass through Mr. Dinnisen's law firm."

"Were they robbing me?"

"I don't think so. It's just that your clone was not the most trusting soul I've ever encountered." Suddenly Egan smiled. "We were able to imprint your personality and memories on him."

"Who is this Kinoshita?" asked Nighthawk. "I never heard of him."

"He trained your first clone. The second one didn't really require any training, but Kinoshita accompanied him on his mission."

"Is he still around?"

"I believe so."

"And he's still got my money?"

"No. He deposited it in his own bank with instructions that they were to continue making payments to us, and were to release whatever remained only to you after you were cured."

"He sounds like a good man," said Nighthawk. "Pass the word that I want to see him after all this surgery is done."

"I'll contact him now. Your recovery will be a long, painful process. You could use a friend in the weeks to come."

"Just do what I said," replied Nighthawk, fighting back a surge of nausea and dizziness.

Egan nodded. "And now, if we have nothing further to discuss, I think it's time I transferred you to the hospital."

"Good," said Nighthawk. "The sooner we get this over with, the sooner I can do the two things I most want to do."

"What are they?" asked Egan curiously.

"Eat without getting sick, and look in a mirror without flinching."

Chapter 2

♦ ♦ ♦ ♦ ♦ ♦ ♦

The small man entered the hospital room and walked to the foot of Nighthawk's bed. There were half a dozen tubes running into the old man's body, some dripping medication, some supplying nourishment, one delivering the recently synthesized enzyme that would finally trigger the cure to his *eplasia*.

"Who the hell are you?" demanded Nighthawk.

"My name is Ito Kinoshita."

Nighthawk instinctively extended a hand, saw the bones of his knuckles protruding through the rotted skin, and pulled it back, hiding it beneath the light blanket that covered him. "I'm told I owe you a debt of gratitude."

Kinoshita shook his head. "It was a pleasure to work with you." He paused. "Well, a version of you."

"You worked with both clones?"

"Not really. All I did with the first one was train

him as best I could, and then they sent him out alone."
Kinoshita frowned. "I warned them that he wasn't ready,
but they wouldn't listen."

"Killed the first day out?" suggested Nighthawk.

"No, he was *you* at age twenty-three. He had your
abilities, your instincts. Nobody could kill him."

"Then, what happened?"

"Innocence. Ignorance. Hormones." Kinoshita
shrugged. "You name it."

"I don't understand," said Nighthawk.

"Physically he was twenty-three. But in actuality
he was two months old. He had your skills, but not your
experience. He didn't know whom to trust and whom
not to, he couldn't spot a woman who was using him or
a man who was conning him, and it cost him his life.
He lasted a lot longer than I thought he would—long
enough to fulfill his mission—but he was doomed from
the day they created him."

"If he did what he was supposed to do, why was
there a second clone?"

"Inflation," answered Kinoshita. "The money the
first clone was paid bought you two extra years, but it
took longer to come up with the cure for your disease,
and the planet's inflation rate is running at twenty-
two percent. There was nothing in the initial agreement
that allowed your attorneys to dip into capital, and the
medics wouldn't give them permission to awaken you.
When the interest could no longer pay the bills, that
would be the end of it—so they had to accept another
commission on your behalf or you'd have been turned
out."

"Tell me about the second clone," said Nighthawk.
"You traveled with him?"

"By the time they created him, they'd found a
way to give him all your memories." Kinoshita looked
into the past and smiled. "There was never anything
like him—except you, of course," he added hastily. "I
remember once he was surrounded by a couple of

hundred angry men on a planet called Cellestra. All I
could think of was that those men were in a lot more
trouble than they realized."

"Where is he now?"

"I've no idea. If he survived, he was going to go
out to the Rim."

"*If* he survived?"

"We found a lot of evidence pointing to his death,"
said Kinoshita. "But he was so . . . so *indestructible* that I
think he must have planted it to hide his tracks."

"And he gave you some money before that?"

"More than 'some,' " answered Kinoshita. "It's been
keeping you alive for almost three years. Once you're
out of the hospital, what remains of the principal is en-
tirely yours."

"What do I owe you for your services?"

"I don't want anything. It was an honor to serve
the Widowmaker." He looked meaningfully at Nighthawk. "It will be again, if you'll let me."

"The Widowmaker's history," said Nighthawk. "I'm
a sixty-two-year-old man who's been on ice for more
than a century. I don't know what this era is like."

"Neither did your clone, sir—but *he* adjusted."

"*He* had a mission," came the answer. "Me, I just
want to enjoy being alive and healthy."

"What do you plan to do?"

Nighthawk shrugged. "Probably find some quiet
backwater world and buy a few acres. Get myself a wife.
Maybe grow some flowers. Catch up on my reading."

"A man like you?" said Kinoshita. "I don't believe it."

"What you believe is of no concern to me. I've
been dying for a century and a quarter, and suddenly
I've been given life and some semblance of health. I
plan to spend the remainder of my years reveling in
that gift."

"Well, I'm sure you mean it now . . ."

"You don't even know me," said Nighthawk. "What
do you think gives you an insight into my plans?"

"I know you better than you think," responded

Kinoshita. "I spent months with your second clone. Physically he was in his late thirties, but he had all the memories you have now—or, rather, that you had prior to waking up this last time. His foibles, his personality, his mind—they were all yours. He wasn't just *like* you. He *was* you." Kinoshita paused again. "And he had a partnership with Death the way most priests think they have with God. You may think you want flowers, but they're not for the Widowmaker."

"I told you . . ."

"I know what you told me. But you're the best there is, maybe the best there ever was. You were never an outlaw. You were a lawman and a bounty hunter. The men you killed deserved to die, and you never broke the law. I don't think you can turn your back on your God-given talent. It might even be sinful to contemplate it."

"Mr. Kinoshita . . ." began Nighthawk.

"Ito."

"Ito, then," he continued. "I can barely hold a fork in my hand, let alone a Burner or a Screecher. The bathroom's maybe twelve feet from my bed; I can't walk to it without help. I've been talking to you for about ten minutes; it's probably the longest I've been able to stay awake since they unfroze me. Whatever talent I once had is gone, and a sixty-two-year-old cripple with atrophied muscles isn't likely to get it back."

"You'll get it back," said Kinoshita with total confidence. "After all, you're the Widowmaker."

"I've made enough widows for one lifetime," said Nighthawk, leaning his head back on his pillow and closing his eyes. "I don't want to hear that word again."

"Whatever you say," replied Kinoshita. He watched the old man's chest rising and filling rhythmically, then added softly: "But you can't stop being what you are."

Chapter 3

Nighthawk wiped the sweat from his face without break-ing stride.

"Faster," he said.

The doctor looked up from the treadmill con-trols. "I think you've done enough for one day, Mr. Nighthawk."

"You heard me."

"But—"

"Faster," he repeated.

The doctor shrugged and increased the speed. "The galaxy can wait an extra few weeks for the Widow-maker to make his reappearance," she said. "You're push-ing yourself too hard."

"If I can keep pace, then I'm not pushing too hard. And if I can't, I'll fall off the damned thing soon enough and then you can say that you told me so."

"But what's the rush?"

"If you'd been lying flat on your back for a century, wouldn't *you* be in a hurry?" shot back Nighthawk.

"It's not as if you're in some kind of a race," she noted.

"All my life I had certain physical skills," said Nighthawk, forcing his legs to keep up with the treadmill. "During the past few years—make that the last few years before I submitted myself to the freezing process—I watched them desert me, one by one. I want them back."

"You're sixty-two years old. Surely you don't plan on being a bounty hunter again."

"I don't plan on ever firing another weapon again if I can help it."

"Then I don't see—"

"I want to know that I can if I have to."

"Then you should be practicing at a target range, not a treadmill."

"I also used to walk for miles. Maybe I'll never walk farther than from here to the front door of this place, but I'm not willing to give up that skill just because it's not vital to my existence. Why bother to read? You can live just as long without it. Why listen to music? It never increased anyone's life span." He paused, as more sweat poured down his face. "I want to be Jefferson Nighthawk again, not just some undernourished ghost who's pretending to be him. Does that make any sense to you?"

"Of course it does," she responded. "But I still don't see why you can't become the Jefferson Nighthawk you used to be in easy, reasonable stages, rather than risk hurting yourself. You're not fit."

"Because I admire excellence," said Nighthawk.

"What does *that* have to do with anything?" she asked, confused.

"When I was the Widowmaker, I wasn't just a competent bounty hunter. I wasn't just good with my weapons. I was the best! I worked at what I did and what I was until I couldn't get any better. That's the way I'm made, and I won't settle for being anything less than the best sixty-two-year-old Jefferson Nighthawk I can be."

"That's what I'm trying to help you be."

He shook his head, starting to pant from the exertion. "No. You're trying to help me be a reasonably fit and healthy old man. I'm trying to be Jefferson Nighthawk"—he gasped for breath—"and Jefferson Nighthawk doesn't *settle*."

"He may not settle, but he gets red in the face, and his blood pressure gets too high, and he gets tired," said the doctor. "Let me turn off the treadmill."

"Don't touch it," said Nighthawk in a voice that had convinced more than one outlaw that surrender was the better part of valor.

"All right," she said, walking to the door. "If I don't hear you fall off, I'll be back in five minutes."

"Ten," he grated as she left.

"I thought you were going to raise flowers," remarked Kinoshita as he entered Nighthawk's room.

"I am."

"So why are you lifting weights?"

Nighthawk allowed himself the luxury of a smile. "You can never tell how deep the roots might be."

Kinoshita stared at the weights. "What are you up to now?"

"Forty pounds in each hand."

"Not bad."

"Not good."

"You've only been awake a month," said Kinoshita. "They spent three weeks curing your eplasia, and you've already undergone the first of your cosmetic surgeries. Given what you've undergone just since they brought you back, I'm surprised you can lift *five* pounds in each hand, let alone forty."

"The last surgery is scheduled for five weeks from

today," said Nighthawk. "I plan to be in good enough shape to leave this place the day they finish."

"Are you talking about killing shape or walking-out shape?"

"They're one and the same."

Kinoshita sat down and grinned.

"What's so funny?" demanded Nighthawk.

"You know why I'm here?" responded Kinoshita.

"I haven't the slightest idea."

"The doctors are afraid you're going to work yourself to the point of physical collapse, and that your system has had so many shocks it might not be able to stand another."

"And you find that amusing, do you?" asked Nighthawk, continuing to raise and lower the weights. "Did my clones ever comment on your sense of humor?"

"What's amusing is that they asked me to speak to you. You have no family or close friends, and no one *really* knows you—but at least I knew your clones." He chuckled. "As if anyone who knew them would even *try* to talk you out of something you wanted to do."

"So you're not going to try?"

"Hey, I'm a fan," Kinoshita assured him. "Whatever you want to do is okay with me."

"Then why did you agree to come?"

"I figured if I didn't, they'd just get someone else who doesn't know that you don't argue with the Widowmaker." He grinned. "The hospital's got enough patients. They don't need another one."

"You're brighter than you look," said Nighthawk.

"Thanks."

"That wasn't necessarily a compliment."

Kinoshita stared approvingly at Nighthawk, who stood before a mirror, inspecting his face. The cheekbones still protruded where the flesh had been removed and not yet replaced, but the rest appeared to be reasonably healthy.

"Not bad," said Kinoshita. "A little older, a few more lines, but unquestionably Jefferson Nighthawk."

"A lot of it's second-generation Nighthawk. They took some skin scrapings, put them in a nutrient solution, did God knows what miracles to them, and then gave me new eyelids and a new nose. And my left ear's artificial, too."

"You can hardly call them artificial if they've got your DNA."

"They aren't the ones I was born with," said Nighthawk. "What would you call them?"

"Improvements," answered Kinoshita promptly.

"Not really," said Nighthawk. "A while back, there was a killer on the Inner Frontier called the One-Armed Bandit. Had a prosthetic arm that doubled as a laser rifle. Now, *he* had an improvement. All I've got are second-generation facial features. My eyes can't see into the infrared spectrum, my ears can't hear ultrasonic radio waves, my nose can't pick up the nurses' perfume. The only difference is that this week most of the staff doesn't wince when they look at my face."

"Don't belittle it," said Kinoshita. "That's a hell of a difference."

"Yeah, I suppose so."

"Besides, if you want 'improvements,' you can always get them. You're a rich man."

Nighthawk sighed. "I don't think my body can handle too many more operations. I'm not twenty-five anymore, or even fifty."

"And when you get right down to it, very few gardeners need a laser rifle instead of a green thumb."

"Point taken."

"So where do we plan to settle down and do our gardening?"

"We?"

Kinoshita nodded. "I used to think I was pretty good at my job until they hired me to train you—or, rather, your clones. I knew in less than a minute that I'd never seen anything like you, that I could work the rest of my life and never measure up. For a while it did pretty serious things to my ego, but then I saw what kind of work ethic was required to reach that level of accomplishment." He paused and sighed deeply. "I'm not made that way. I can admire what you do without aspiring to it—or without being willing to make the sacrifices you make to achieve it. So I'm willing to carry your bags, or hoe your garden, or answer your door, or do anything else to stay close enough to you to remind me why I'm *not* a lawman or a bounty hunter anymore. I figure I'll live a lot longer this way."

"I don't remember saying that I *wanted* company."

"You don't know it, but you *owe* me," said Kinoshita. "I sacrificed a lot for you—a whole career."

"I thought you wanted to live to a ripe old age. That's not in the cards for most lawmen."

"I could have made a substantial living as a trainer of lawmen, but your goddamned lawyers blacklisted me after I refused to turn your money over to them— which is probably the only reason you're alive today."

Nighthawk stared at him for a long moment. "All right," he said at last. "You're hired."

"As what?"

"Whatever I need: bodyguard, manservant, cook."

Kinoshita suddenly looked uncomfortable. "So what do I do now?" he said awkwardly.

Nighthawk considered for a moment. "Right now I need a barber. Give me a shave."

"A shave?" repeated Kinoshita, surprised.

"Right. If my face isn't attached properly, I want to know about it *before* I leave for the Frontier."

"You all packed?" asked Kinoshita, entering the hospital room for the last time.

"I don't have any possessions," replied Nighthawk. "I gave them all away a century ago."

Kinoshita laid a light blue outfit down on the bed. "I brought this for you."

Nighthawk made no attempt to hide his distaste. "Ugly," he muttered disapprovingly.

"It's the style—and besides, you'd look silly walking down the street in a hospital gown."

Nighthawk took off his gown and began getting dressed.

"Very impressive," said Kinoshita, looking at his lean, hard body. "You look like a heavyweight freehand fighter who's starved himself down to middleweight for a money fight. The muscles are there, but everything else is gone."

"I'll put the rest of my weight back on," Nighthawk assured him. "They didn't give me enough calories to compensate for all the exercising I did."

"Why didn't you ask for more?"

"I did. Once."

"And?"

"They didn't bring it."

"Why didn't you complain?"

"I don't beg," said Nighthawk, fastening his tunic. He straightened up. "How do I look?"

"Like an older version of the two clones," said Kinoshita. Suddenly he grinned. "I can't imagine why."

"Your sense of humor leaves a lot to be desired."

"By the way, I didn't bring you any weapons," said Kinoshita. "They're illegal on Deluros."

"What do I want a weapon for?"

"You're the Widowmaker."

"That was a long time ago."

"You are what you are."

"I think I prefer your humor to your philosophy." Nighthawk walked to the door and stepped out into the corridor. "Okay, let's go see what the galaxy looks like after all this time."

Chapter 4

$\blacklozenge \quad \blacklozenge \quad \blacklozenge \quad \blacklozenge \quad \blacklozenge \quad \blacklozenge \quad \blacklozenge \quad \blacklozenge$

It was a little house, small and neat, with white-painted walls, a green roof, a brick chimney, and an old-fashioned veranda with a swing and a rocking chair on it. Nighthawk knew the moment his vehicle pulled up in front of the house that he was going to buy it.

"But it's all trees and ravines," protested Kinoshita. "These are not the most productive two hundred acres I've ever seen. Even if you clear them, you can't farm them."

"Then we won't have to work very hard growing things, will we?" responded Nighthawk. He walked around to the side of the house. "We'll put a little pond right here, I think, and stick a few fish in it."

"We passed a river a mile back. It looked like there'd be good fishing there."

"Those fish are for eating. These will be for looking at." Nighthawk continued walking, then came to a stop near the corner of the house. "The garden'll be right here," he said, outlining a space with his hand.

"That's maybe ten feet by twenty," noted Kinoshita glumly. "Maybe less."

"It's big enough for me." He paused. "How deep did they say the well was?"

"Sixty feet."

"Okay," said Nighthawk. "Buy it."

"Don't you want to see the inside?" asked Kinoshita, surprised.

"One house is pretty much like another. If something needs fixing or changing, we'll fix or change it. Besides, I plan to spend most of my time sitting out here on the veranda."

"But—"

"Do it," said Nighthawk so softly that Kinoshita barely heard him and so firmly that all thoughts of protest vanished from the smaller man's mind. Nighthawk walked back to the vehicle. "Drop me at the bar back in town. I'll wait for you there while you take care of the details."

"Do you want a mortgage?"

Nighthawk shook his head. "Buy it outright. I don't like being beholden to anyone."

Kinoshita began driving the vehicle back down the winding, unpaved road. "I wish I knew what you find so charming about dirt roads and ancient houses. Hell, this planet doesn't even have fusion power yet! I thought we were buying a gentleman's farm on Pollux IV or some other major world, not a shack on some little dirtball nobody's ever heard of."

"I've seen my share of worlds. This one'll do."

"Tell me that when we run out of water, or the roof collapses from the snow."

"No one says you have to stay here," replied Nighthawk. "Take a third of the money and leave."

"And go where?" demanded Kinoshita.

"Someplace you like better."

"Not a chance," said Kinoshita adamantly. "I'm staying with you."

"Then shut up and drive. I'm an old man, and I haven't got the energy to argue."

They drove the next six miles in silence and finally reached the small town that had sprung up around Churchill II's primitive landing field. Then Kinoshita pulled to a stop in front of a nondescript tavern.

"It shouldn't take more than about ten minutes to transfer the funds, and maybe another five to transfer the title. I'll be back in fifteen or twenty minutes unless there's a hitch."

"I'll be here," said Nighthawk, getting out of the vehicle and walking into the tavern.

Force of habit made him pick out a table in the darkest corner of the room, and to sit with his back to the wall, so that he could see the doorway and the windows.

The table glowed and came to life. A holograph listing all the drinks available hovered in front of him, and a mechanical voice asked him to make a selection.

"Beer."

"We have two hundred and eighty-four brands from seventy-three worlds. You must be more specific."

"Have you got any local brews?"

"There are no breweries on Churchill II."

"Then select one for me."

"I am not programmed to perform that function."

"You can't randomize?"

"No I cannot, sir. If I were to select a brand you do not like, there is a fifty-seven-percent probability that you would refuse to pay for it. Our profit margin is forty-two percent. If I randomize for you, I must randomize for everyone—and if I select beer for everybody, the mathematical likelihood is that we will lose money on more than half our transactions."

"All right," said Nighthawk. "Give me whatever you've sold the most of today."

An instant later the top of the table irised right in front of him, and a tall glass of beer appeared just before the surface became solid again.

"That will be four credits, or one Maria Theresa dollar, or five Far London shillings, or . . ."

Nighthawk pressed his hand down on the table. "Read my thumbprint and bill my account on Deluros VIII."

"Reading . . . done." The mechanical voice was silent for a moment. Then: "Potential error."

"What's the problem?"

"You are Jefferson Nighthawk?"

"That's right."

"According to the Master Credit Computer on Deluros VIII, you are one hundred and seventy-four years old. My data banks tell me that no human, even of mutated stock, has ever lived past one hundred and forty-seven years."

"Well, now you'll have something to add to your data banks, won't you?"

"Have I your permission to read your retinagram?"

"Seems like a lot of trouble for four credits."

"Have I your permission to read your retinagram?" repeated the machine emotionlessly.

"Yeah, go ahead."

"Ready . . . checking . . . cross-checking . . . confirming. You *are* Jefferson Nighthawk."

"Fancy that," said Nighthawk, finally picking up his beer and taking a long swallow.

He sat in silence, observing his surroundings with an expert eye. Three middle-aged men sat at a table near the door, eating sandwiches they had brought with them and drinking beer. A young man whose clothes were too bright and whose weapon was too new and shiny stood at the bar, drinking some blue concoction. As he did so, the ice cubes, which were obviously not made of water, chimed musically. A woman sat as far from the men as possible, staring severely at the small glass in front of her.

Nighthawk nursed his beer, relishing the feel of the place, of not being on Deluros with its mile-high buildings and its thirty-three billion inhabitants. A small insect began crawling across the table. He considered killing it, then changed his mind, leaned back, and waited a few seconds for the table to sense, pinpoint, and atomize it.

The young man glanced over, momentarily attracted by the power surge in the table, and their eyes met. Nighthawk stared at him, calm and unblinking, and soon the young man frowned and turned away uncomfortably, as if he was not used to having people meet his gaze.

"Let's have something to watch!" snapped the young man.

"I possess a library of one thousand six hundred fifty-two sporting events, three thousand five hundred sixty-six dramatic entertainments, four hundred two documentaries . . ."

"There must have been a championship fight somewhere in the Oligarchy last week. Let's have it."

Instantly a life-sized holograph of two almost-naked men, their hands and feet heavily taped, appeared above the bar. They began circling each other, feinting and punching, throwing an occasional kick.

The fight was a dull one, with each party showing too much respect for the other's ability, and Nighthawk was glad when it ended some ten minutes later and the images vanished.

"Another," said the young man.

Nighthawk, who had no desire to watch another match, was about to get up and leave the tavern when Kinoshita walked through the doorway, looked around until he spotted him, and then walked over to his table.

"Any problems?" asked Nighthawk.

"None," answered Kinoshita. "Everything went smoothly. You now own an exceptional ugly house on two hundred useless acres. I hope you're thrilled."

"Satisfied, anyway."

"Since we're in a tavern, I suppose we might as well celebrate with a drink."

"Be my guest."

"What kind of beer did you have?"

Nighthawk, shrugged. "Beats me."

"Any good?"

"It's decent enough."

"Two more beers," ordered Kinoshita.

"Cancel that," said Nighthawk as the table glowed with artificial life again.

"Canceled," said a mechanical voice.

"Make that one beer, same kind, and give me whatever that young man at the bar had. The blue drink that seemed to play a melody."

The young man suddenly looked up. "Cancel that," he said, swaggering over to the table.

"Have you got a problem, son?" asked Kinoshita.

"Who told you that you could order my drink, old man?" said the young man, never taking his eyes from Nighthawk.

"Do you know who you're talking to?" demanded Kinoshita.

"An old man who ordered something that's not his," came the answer. "Do you know who you're talking to? I'm Johnny Trouble." He continued staring at Nighthawk. "Ever hear of me?"

"I've heard of four or five Johnny Troubles."

"Yeah?" said Johnny Trouble, surprised.

Nighthawk nodded. "And a couple of Billy Troubles, too. They were all much deeper into the Frontier."

"How come I never heard of 'em?"

"It was before your time," said Nighthawk. He paused, then added: "And they all died young."

"Well, I'm Johnny Trouble now, and there's only one of me."

"Whatever you say."

"Take my word for it, one's enough," said Johnny Trouble. "Maybe you heard that the Widowmaker showed up a couple of years ago. I made him back down." Nighthawk found that thought amusing, and the young man glared at him suspiciously. "What are you smiling about?"

"I'm just happy that a man of your caliber is protecting my new world," replied Nighthawk easily. "Now can I order my drink?"

"I'm the guy who created it. It's mine. No one orders it without my permission."

"Whatever makes you happy," said Nighthawk. "May I have your permission?"

"What's it worth to you?"

Nighthawk sighed deeply. "Not as much as you think," he replied, getting slowly to his feet and holding his hands out from his body in plain view. "We don't want any trouble. We'll take our business elsewhere."

Kinoshita sat there, stunned.

"Come on, Ito," said Nighthawk. "We've upset this gentleman enough already."

Kinoshita stood up and followed Nighthawk to the door, while the young man, smiling smugly, stood in the center of the floor, hands on hips, watching them go.

"Are you all right?" asked Kinoshita when they were both outside and the door had shut behind them.

"Yeah, I'm fine."

"I wonder. The Nighthawks I knew would have taken that kid's gun away and pistol-whipped him with it."

"The Nighthawks you knew were twenty-three and thirty-eight years old. I've been dead for more than a century. It doesn't take that much of an effort to step aside when someone like that kid in there is feeling his testosterone."

"What if he'd pulled his gun?"

"He'd have killed me. I'm unarmed—and even if I *was* packed, I haven't held a weapon in my hands in a hundred and twelve years. It wouldn't have been much of a contest."

"So you're just going to withdraw from the world, and back down whenever someone challenges you?"

"I'm sixty-two years old. It's the best way I know to make it to seventy-two."

"I can't believe I'm speaking to the Widowmaker."

"You're not," said Nighthawk firmly. "Not anymore."

They reached the vehicle. "Where to now?" asked Kinoshita.

"Let's go home," said Nighthawk. Suddenly he smiled. "Let's go home," he said again.

"What's so funny?"

"I just realized that I've never had one before." He looked down the road. "It's about time. Let's go home." Then he nodded. "Yeah, I like the sound of it."

Chapter 5

◆ ◆ ◆ ◆ ◆ ◆ ◆ ◆

Knowing what a perfectionist the second clone had been, Kinoshita expected Nighthawk to spend weeks, perhaps months, of intensive effort on the house until it exactly suited his tastes, but instead the older man bought some nondescript furniture and paid no further attention to the interior, except to spend one afternoon building a set of bookcases.

"No one reads books anymore," protested Kinoshita as he watched Nighthawk carefully creating the shelves.

"*I* do."

"That's silly. You can call up any book ever written on your computer."

"I don't have a computer."

"Then we'll buy one the next time we go into town."

"I don't *like* computers. I like the heft and feel and smell of a book."

"Do you know how much they cost?" demanded Kinoshita.

"I've got thousands of them stashed all over the Frontier," answered Nighthawk. "Damned near every place I've ever lived. I'll send for them one of these days."

"I think we'd better get you a computer anyway."

"Can it chop wood, or plant flowers, or light a fire?"

"Of course not."

"Then I don't want it and I don't need it," said Nighthawk decisively.

"Don't you want to know what's going on in the galaxy?" asked Kinoshita.

"Absolutely not. I'm retired, remember?"

"Are you retired from bounty hunting or from life?"

"A little of each, I think."

"You're getting into a rut."

"It's a rut I like."

And it *was* a pleasant enough rut. Every morning Nighthawk rose, forced himself to have breakfast—a meal he detested—and then spent the better part of an hour chopping wood. The house had both solar and nuclear heating systems, but Nighthawk enjoyed sitting by a fire, and he refused to sit in front of an artificial one.

At least, that was the reason he gave, and it was probably a valid one—but Kinoshita also noticed that he was adding muscle to his spare frame almost daily.

He also fetched a few gallons of water from the river each day, and Kinoshita *knew* that was to regain strength in his legs, since the house had three different water sources.

In the afternoons he went out hunting. The first five days he came back empty-handed, but after that he never failed to bring back something for the pot. There were some large herbivores in the nearby woods, five-hundred-pounders, but Nighthawk invariably brought home the amazingly quick, shifty little five-pound rabbit-like creatures that lived near the river. They made decent enough eating, but what it meant to Kinoshita was that the Widowmaker's aim and reflexes were back.

"Not bad," said Kinoshita, looking up from his most recent dinner. They took turns cooking, and this meal had been prepared by Nighthawk.

"I like the sauce," replied Nighthawk. "An Emran showed me how to make it, back on Silverdew."

"Still," continued Kinoshita, "don't you get a little tired of eating the same thing every day?"

"I ate the same thing every day for decades."

"What are you talking about?"

"Soya products," answered Nighthawk. "Oh, they all taste different, but they're essentially the same thing." He paused. "You set foot on a couple of hundred different worlds with different gravities and atmospheres, your body has enough adjusting to do. There's no sense overloading it with alien food, too."

"You were a careful man."

"Careless young men don't live to be careless old men, not in my profession."

"Do you miss it?"

"Soya food?"

"No. Your profession."

Nighthawk shook his head. "Not at all."

"It doesn't make sense," said Kinoshita. "You were the best there ever was."

"Oh, I doubt it."

"Who was better?"

Nighthawk lowered his head in thought for a moment, then looked up. "They say there was nobody as good as Peacemaker MacDougal and the Angel. And whoever killed Conrad Bland back on Walpurgis III had to be pretty good, too, considering the odds."

"That was thousands of years ago!" protested Kinoshita.

"I wasn't aware there was a time limit on being the best," responded Nighthawk with a wry smile. "You know, there was a carnival performer—I don't know if he really existed—who was supposed to be the best shot who ever lived. Can't recall his name—Singer, Jumper, something like that."

"Billybuck Dancer?"

"Yeah, that was it."

"I saw a statue of him back on Kargennian II," said Kinoshita. "It's covered with birdshit and graffiti, and part of it's crumbled away, but I could still make out the name at the base. Still, you can't help wondering how good he'd have been against something that could shoot back."

"Who knows?" answered Nighthawk. "Legend has it that he got killed in a gunfight." He paused. "Of course, sooner or later we all do."

"Not you," said Kinoshita adamantly.

"Even me."

"Not a chance. I've been watching you get yourself into shape," said Kinoshita. "You're almost ready."

Nighthawk shook his head. "You know the difference between a kid like Johnny Trouble and me? He's too young to know he can be killed. He never thinks about it. When he's in a fight, images of what could happen don't flash through his mind and make him pause. That's why all the killers out here are young. Once you realize that you can lose your life, you also start realizing just how precious it is. That makes you think, and thinking makes you hesitate, and you know what happens to he who hesitates."

"I spent months with your second clone," said Kinoshita, unimpressed. "He was physically thirty-eight, but he had your memories. Mentally and emotionally he was sixty-two. So why didn't he hesitate?"

"You'd have to ask him."

"I'm asking you. It's the same thing."

"Not quite. He was in perfect health, and he knew that they'd develop the cure for eplasia before he was riddled with it."

"Apples and oranges," protested Kinoshita. "He was sixty-two mentally, and he didn't hesitate."

"He had special knowledge."

"What special knowledge?"

"He knew that when he was in his fifties, he was still taking out twenty-two-year-old kids. Very few thirty-eight-year-olds have the absolute knowledge that they won't lose a nanosecond off their reflexes for another decade or more." Nighthawk sighed. "But I'm sixty-two, and I've been frozen for a century, and half my skin is artificial, and I know I'll never again be what I was."

"Okay, I concede," said Kinoshita. "But you still haven't really answered me: Do you miss the excitement?"

"Nothing very exciting about hunting down scum. You were a lawman. Did *you* find it exciting?"

"No, but . . ."

"But what?"

"But I wasn't the Widowmaker."

"Well, I'm not, either. I'm just Jefferson Nighthawk."

"I don't understand you at all. When you're the best at something . . ."

"You know what I was the best at?" said Nighthawk irritably. "I was the best at scaring women and children. I'd walk down the street, and they'd see my skin flaking off in front of their eyes, my bones jutting through it, and I'd give them nightmares for months to come." He paused. "After a while I started wearing gloves and a mask, so no one would have to see the effects of my disease. But word had gotten out. Young men didn't have to prove how tough they were by going up against me; now they proved it by trying to steal my mask so they could look at my face without getting sick—and not a hell of a lot of them were able to." Nighthawk's face twisted into a grimace as he paused for breath. "*That's* the Widowmaker's legacy—along with hundreds of terrified women and children, I could make strong men sick to their stomachs just by walking into a room."

"I'm sorry," said Kinoshita. "I hadn't realized . . ."

"It's all right," replied Nighthawk. "It's over now. And so is the Widowmaker."

"What made you finally choose to freeze yourself?"

"A doctor out on Binder X gave me six weeks to live, eight at the outside. I'd grown accustomed to scaring everyone who saw me, but I wasn't ready to die. He suggested that since I was sitting on a few million credits I check myself into the cryonics lab on Deluros VIII and wait for a cure. He thought it was maybe forty years off; he was seventy-two years short. Must be one hell of a disease."

"It was."

"I hope my clone got cured."

"He had enough money. I'm sure he did." Kinoshita paused. "Do you really plan to find him?"

Nighthawk shook his head. "What for? If he wanted to see me, he'd have left word. He did what he was created to do. If he wants to create a new identity and be left alone, I'll honor his wishes."

Nighthawk got up, cleaned off the table, and went outside to sit on a rocking chair.

"Lots of stars out tonight," he remarked when Kinoshita finally joined him.

Kinoshita looked up. "Lots of *worlds*." He paused. "I'll bet some of them are pretty interesting."

"I've seen a lot of worlds," said Nighthawk. "This one'll do as well as any."

"Are you just going to chop wood and hunt and fish all day, every day, forever?"

"Sounds good to me."

"Sounds boring as hell to me."

"Well, I'll be reading, too."

"How exciting."

"It's about all the excitement I can handle these days," said Nighthawk with a smile.

"And that's really all you plan to do?"

"Well, I've been thinking of joining a church."

Kinoshita laughed out loud. "You? The man who's

sent a couple of hundred men and aliens straight to hell?"

"Yeah, me."

"Any particular religion?"

"Nope."

"Then why join?" persisted Kinoshita.

"Best place I can think of to meet a nice middle-aged widow woman."

"You want to get married?"

"I've lived alone all my life," answered Nighthawk. "I can't see much to recommend it."

"Aren't you a little old to change?"

Nighthawk shrugged. "Mankind adapts; that's what we do better than any other species." He leaned back on his chair. "I might be a little old to be sporting a young man's passion, but that doesn't mean I don't want to spend my final years with someone I care for." He paused and turned to his companion. "Nothing personal, but you aren't what I have in mind."

"I think I can live without being lusted after by the Widowmaker," answered Kinoshita with a laugh. "But if I can ask: Why a church?"

"I've spent a lot of time in bars and drug dens and whorehouses and gambling parlors, and I haven't seen an awful lot of women my age in them."

"Did you ever consider marrying a young one?"

Nighthawk shook his head. "Never once."

"Why not?"

"It's annoying enough having to put up with your less-than-subtle hints that I should go back to being the Widowmaker. I don't need some twenty-year-old wife looking for that same vicarious excitement."

"I'm not looking for vicarious excitement," said Kinoshita defensively.

"If you say so," answered Nighthawk, closing his eyes and rocking gently in his chair.

They sat in silence for almost half an hour. Then Kinoshita gently nudged him.

"Jefferson!" he whispered. "There's a Nightkiller about two hundred yards away, just beside that big tree."

"I know," answered Nighthawk softly. "I've been watching it for about ten minutes now. Looks more canine than feline, despite the fact that it can climb trees."

"Do you want to borrow my Burner or my Screecher?" asked Kinoshita.

"He's not bothering anyone," said Nighthawk. "And I'm tired of killing."

The Nightkiller, alerted by the sound of their voices, glared at them for a moment, then slunk off into the darkness.

"I hope he remembers you gave him a pass," said Kinoshita.

"He won't bother us."

"You think not?"

"We're not native to this world. He doesn't recognize us as prey."

"You go out hunting every day," Kinoshita pointed out. "He may recognize you as a competitor."

"There's food enough for all of us."

"He's only an animal. He may not be able to reason it out."

"Then I'll worry about it when the time comes."

Kinoshita looked at the old man, who had closed his eyes again and was rocking gently in his chair.

You were the greatest. I suppose if you want to spend the rest of your life stuck on this backwater world, that's not too much to ask, given all that you've accomplished. Who am I to insist that you keep bucking the odds until they finally catch up with you? I won't call you Widowmaker again.

Chapter 6

● ● ● ● ● ● ● ● ●

◈

Kinoshita was awakened the next morning by the sound of the older man chopping wood.

"Good morning," said Nighthawk as Kinoshita stepped outside, shielding his eyes from the glare of the sun.

"You didn't wake me for breakfast."

"We'll eat in town. I've got some supplies to buy."

"Supplies?"

"Spices for the kitchen, seeds for the garden. Maybe a couple of new tunics; the ones I've got are getting a bit tight in the shoulders."

"Let me shave and shower and I'll be right with you."

"Tell you what," said Nighthawk. "I can use a little exercise." He buried his ax in a tree stump. "I'll start walking. You can pick me up along the way."

"Whatever you say," answered Kinoshita, idly

wondering how many men Nighthawk's age could chop wood for an hour and then walk five miles into town.

Kinoshita took a long, leisurely, hot shower, atomized the hairs on his face, had a quick cup of coffee, and then set out for town in their vehicle. He caught up with Nighthawk after four miles.

"I thought maybe you'd gone back to sleep," said the older man as he climbed onto the passenger's seat.

"You said you wanted some exercise," replied Kinoshita defensively. He looked over. "Your shirt's drenched. I didn't think you could work up that kind of sweat from walking along a tree-shaded dirt road."

"Actually, I jogged for a couple of miles."

"You did?"

"Yeah." A guilty smile. "I didn't want anyone to see me in case I couldn't make it."

"You're getting into shape, no question about it," said Kinoshita. "Forgive me for asking, but just what are you getting into shape *for*?"

"I depended on my body for half a century, and it never betrayed me, never let me down," answered Nighthawk. "I never worried about stamina, or overweight, or blood pressure, or diabetes, or anything else. Then it proved as frail as everyone else's, and now that I've got a second chance, I plan to keep it in as good a condition as I can." He looked across at Kinoshita. "That's it. No hidden agenda, no secret goal. I've been deathly ill; now I just want to stay healthy."

"No argument," came the answer. "I just wonder, since you're becoming such a fanatic on the subject, why you haven't nagged *me* to get in better shape?"

"You're health is your own business, not mine."

"Now *that* sounds like the Nighthawk I used to know," said Kinoshita in satisfied tones.

"No reason why it shouldn't. We're the same."

They entered the town, and came to a stop in front of a farm supply store.

"You need me to help you carry anything?" asked

Kinoshita as Nighthawk climbed out. The older man merely stared at him. "Sorry. Silly question."

Nighthawk entered the store and began looking at various displays.

"Morning, Mr. Nighthawk," said the clerk.

"Good morning, Jacob."

"Anything I can help you with?"

"Maybe. There's a brilliant yellow flower that grows on Greenwillow."

"Greenwillow?" repeated Jacob. "Give me a sec." He activated his computer. "Greenwillow."

"Greenwillow," repeated the machine. "Official name: Sunderman II. Location: the Inner Frontier."

"All right, Sunderman II. Yellow flower. Show me what you've got."

Holograms of fourteen flowers, all yellow, appeared in the air above the computer.

"Is it any of these, Mr. Nighthawk?" asked Jacob.

"Third from the left," answered Nighthawk. Jacob pointed to one. "No, *my* left."

"Okay, got it." Jacob uttered a brief command to the computer, read a screen, and looked up. "The local name for it is the Sunspot."

"Right," said Nighthawk. "That's it. How soon can you get me some?"

"How many?"

"Four or five dozen."

"First let me check and make sure it can survive in our soil." He spoke briefly to the machine. "Yes, it can take our gravity and soil. The atmosphere's no problem; neither is the water." He paused as more information appeared. "They're perennials, but a freeze, even a mild one, will wipe 'em out."

"Order them."

"Don't you want to know what the price is, Mr. Nighthawk?" asked Jacob.

"I'm sure you won't jack it up," said Nighthawk. "Just bill my account."

"All right. They'll be here in about a week. Can I help you with anything else?"

"Not today. I've still got to get over to the grocer's and then meet my friend."

"By the way, I saw Johnny Trouble walking around this morning," said the clerk. "I'd be careful. He seems to have taken a real dislike to you."

"Thanks for the warning," said Nighthawk.

He left the store, walked across the street, picked up the spices he wanted, and returned to the vehicle, which was empty. He looked into a couple of restaurant windows, spotted Kinoshita sitting down to an omelet made from imported eggs and mutated ham, and joined him.

"Thanks for waiting," said Nighthawk sardonically.

"I was starving."

"You must have been some lawman. What happened when you got hungry during a hot pursuit?"

"I ate. No sense going up against a killer in a weakened condition."

"A weakened condition is three bullets in your abdomen, or a hand sliced off by a Burner. What you're describing is a hungry condition."

"Make fun of me all you want," said Kinoshita defensively, "but I made it past forty without your skills. I must have done *something* right."

"Yeah," said Nighthawk, smiling. "You stopped for dinner while all the really dangerous outlaws got away."

"Have your fun," said Kinoshita, "but if you start talking about calories and diets, I'm going to get a room in town."

"Hell, eat all you want. Our days of chasing bad guys are over."

"Speaking of which, I saw that young gun going into the bar across the street."

"He starts his drinking early, doesn't he? remarked Nighthawk.

"That's all you have to say?"

"There's no law against getting drunk before noon."

"If he sees you . . ."

"If he sees me, I'll step aside. It doesn't take all that much effort."

"I *still* don't understand you."

"I'm not wearing any weapons," said Nighthawk. "What would you have me do?"

Kinoshita sighed. "Nothing. It's none of my business."

"Right the first time."

Nighthawk called up a menu, made his selections, and ate in silence. Kinoshita kept looking nervously out the window for Johnny Trouble, but Nighthawk paid attention only to the meal in front of him.

When they were done they walked out to the vehicle.

"You want to jog back?" asked Kinoshita.

"I'm an old man," answered Nighthawk, climbing in. "In fact, right now I'm a stiff, tired old man. Two miles a day is plenty."

They had driven about half the distance when Nighthawk asked Kinoshita to stop.

"What is it?"

"That bird up there," said Nighthawk, pointing. "It's lovely. I wonder what it is?"

"What bird where?"

"Right over there. Eleven o'clock, about a quarter mile away. Top branch, to the left of the bole."

Kinoshita peered for a moment, then shook his head. "All I can see is a kind of reddish lump. You can actually make out details?"

"And colors."

"Well, there's sure as hell nothing wrong with your eyes."

"There never was. Eplasia doesn't affect the vision."

"So are you going to become a bird-watcher now?"

"No. It just caught my attention." Nighthawk paused thoughtfully. "You know, I *could* get into birding, now that I come to think of it."

Kinoshita shrugged. "Whatever makes you happy."

"I think a pastoral existence in my old age is what will make me happy. At least, it has so far." Suddenly he peered ahead and frowned.

"What is it?" asked Kinoshita, instantly alert. "What do you see?"

"I'm not sure. But get this thing moving and head for home—fast!"

Kinoshita peeled away on the dirt road.

"Shit!" muttered Nighthawk.

"What's the matter?" demanded Kinoshita, almost losing touch with the road as he raced around a turn.

"Smoke," said Nighthawk. "Plenty of it."

"Coming from near the house?"

"Very."

They sped on for another two miles, then halted fifty yards from the house, which was totally ablaze.

"What the hell could have happened?" demanded Kinoshita, emerging from the vehicle. "Maybe some embers from last night's fire?"

"This wasn't any accident," said Nighthawk grimly. He saw something fluttering from the stump where he had buried his ax, walked over, picked it up, and frowned.

"What is it?" asked Kinoshita, joining him.

"A message," he said, handing it over.

" *'This is for Colonel Hernandez!'* " Kinoshita read aloud.

"Who the hell *is* he?" said Nighthawk. "I never heard of any Colonel Hernandez."

"*I* have," said Kinoshita grimly.

"He's one of yours?"

Kinoshita shook his head. "No, Jefferson. You killed him."

"The hell I did."

"I know," said Kinoshita. "I was there."

Chapter 7

◆ ◆ ◆ ◆ ◆ ◆ ◆ ◆

✦

"Explain!"

"The first clone was created for Colonel James Hernandez of Solio II," answered Kinoshita. "He was the one who instigated the creation of the clone, and he paid the bill."

"Surely I didn't kill him for that?"

"The first clone didn't kill him at all. He—the clone—was as efficient a killer as you were at twenty-three, but mentally and emotionally he was only a few months old. He was naive and innocent, and it cost him his life."

"How?"

"He found out, somehow, that Hernandez was using him for his own ends, and he went to Solio and tried to kill him. I don't know all the details, but I'm told there was a woman involved. Anyway, it was a trap, and it was the clone who died."

"But he killed Hernandez in the process?"

Kinoshita shook his head. "No."

"Then who did?"

"The second clone."

"Did Hernandez pay for the second clone as well?" asked Nighthawk.

"No," said Kinoshita. "The second clone was commissioned by Cassius Hill, the governor of a world named Pericles. But the second clone found out what had happened to his predecessor, and he made it his business to settle accounts on the way to Pericles."

"And *he* killed Hernandez?"

"Right. I know; I was there."

"Then you know who else was there?"

"He shot him in the middle of a crowded restaurant on Solio II. In fact, he killed Hernandez and four or five bodyguards."

"So some survivor spotted one of us and burned the house down."

"What do you mean, 'one of us'?" demanded Kinoshita. "You're the one who killed him."

"I'll wager you've changed a hell of a lot less in the last three years than I have," answered Nighthawk. "I'm still twenty pounds lighter than I was in my prime, my hair is halfway between gray and white, my face is lined. It's much more likely that they recognized you and then doped out who I was."

Kinoshita was silent for a long moment. "You know," he admitted at last, "you've got a point."

"Well, at least you'll be able to identify them when we find them."

"I don't know that for a fact," answered Kinoshita. "I don't know if I could identify everyone who was in that restaurant. Besides, Hernandez was the most powerful man on the planet, and he was as corrupt as hell. If the new regime replaced all his cronies and loyalists, you could have thousands of embittered men and women out for revenge."

"Only half a dozen of which you might possibly

recognize," suggested Nighthawk grimly. "Is that what you're trying to tell me?"

"Yeah, I think that's pretty much it."

Nighthawk stood, hands on hips, watching the last wall of the house collapse. "How much was it insured for?" he asked, surveying the damage.

"About twenty percent of cost."

"No more?"

"The land was worth eighty percent, and you still own it." Kinoshita paused. "Do you want to rebuild?"

"What's the point? They know where I live. They'll just come back."

"So what do we do?"

"We collect the insurance, put the land up for sale, and leave."

"Leave for where?"

"I don't know. We'll go deeper into the Frontier until we find another world."

"Should I get us a room at the hotel in town?" asked Kinoshita.

"Why?"

"I thought you might want to come back in a couple of days, when the ruins have cooled down, and see if there's anything left."

"It was a wood house. What the hell do you think will be left?"

"Well, actually, I was thinking we might find a clue as to who did this."

"I don't much give a damn," said Nighthawk. "If they're in town, you'll point them out to me. If they've already left the planet, I'm not about to spend the rest of my life tracking them down."

"Jefferson Nighthawk's just going to walk away?" demanded Kinoshita disbelievingly.

"Jefferson Nighthawk's going to vanish. I want a new identity before we settle on the next world. I don't plan to be a target for people I can't even recognize." He walked back to the vehicle. "There's nothing we can do here. Let's get going."

"The fire might spread."

"Let it. We're never coming back."

Kinoshita stared thoughtfully at him. *You're no-where near as devastated as you should be. I thought you loved this place, that you wanted to spend the rest of your life here. But if you can just shrug and walk away, I was wrong. You're not quite the Widowmaker yet, or you'd be after whoever did this with blood in your eye; but you're not Jefferson Nighthawk, either, or you'd be more deeply affected. I don't know which one you're going to wind up being; in fact, I don't know which one I want you to be. Yet.*

"Are we just going to sit here all morning?" asked Nighthawk sardonically.

"Sorry," said Kinoshita, ordering the vehicle to accelerate.

"When we get to town, report the fire to the authorities, put in a claim for the insurance, and see if you can buy a new ship. If you can, trade ours in."

"Ours works fine."

"Ours is registered in my name. If there's an easier way to trace a man, I've never found it."

"So what name do you want me to register the new ship in?" asked Kinoshita.

"Shit!" muttered Nighthawk. "I'd forgotten. I won't get a new ID and passport until we're deeper into the Frontier." He sighed deeply. "All right, we'll keep the ship a little longer."

"What are you going to be doing while I'm talking to the insurance company and the police?"

"The fire department, not the police," Nighthawk corrected him.

"But it was arson!" protested Kinoshita.

Nighthawk pulled the message out of a pocket and ripped it to shreds, throwing the pieces out the window. "If they think it was arson, we'll be stuck here for a week, answering questions and filling out forms."

"You're the boss."

"Hold that thought." The vehicle slowed down as they approached the town. "Anyway, in answer to your question, I've got a bunch of things on order, everything from furniture to flowers. I've got to cancel them. And there's something I have to buy." They neared the feed store. "Drop me here. I'll meet you at the bar."

Nighthawk got out of the vehicle, walked into the store, and cancelled the morning's order. He walked up and down the street, doing the same thing at a hardware and a furniture store.

Finally he entered a small shop next to the restaurant.

An old, bald man squinted across the room at him. "I've seen you around, Mr. Nighthawk. Can I help you find something?"

"Probably. Do you handle just new equipment, or do you have some old stuff lying around?"

"Half and half. What are you looking for?"

"I'll know it when I see it," said Nighthawk, starting to examine the display cases. "Pull this one out, please."

"Nice choice. Belonged to a lawman. Kept him alive long enough to retire."

Nighthawk examined the laser pistol, hefted it, checked the sights with an expert eye.

"Power pack?"

"Right there."

"Where?"

"When's the last time you used a Burner?" asked the old man, curious.

"A long time ago," answered Nighthawk.

"It's right there in the handle."

"This?" asked Nighthawk, pointing to the tiny battery.

"Yeah, that's it."

"How long is it good for?"

"Depends how much you're using it. It'll hold up for a twenty-minute blast in a lab. In the field, when you stop and start, probably about half that."

"How much are the batteries?"

"Two hundred credits each. I can take Maria

Theresa dollars or Far London pounds. Word is that
there's been a revolution on New Stalin, so I'm not taking New Stalin rubles this week."

"I'll take the Burner, and a dozen batteries. Got a
holster?"

"New or old?"

"Old. I want one that I know works."

"I can give you the one it came with. It's kind of
ratty, but it'll hold the gun."

"Fine. Now show me your Screechers."

Nighthawk examined eight sonic pistols with an
expert eye, chose the one he wanted, and picked up another dozen batteries fitted to that model.

"Anything else?"

"Something that makes a bang."

"Only got one, and it's brand-new."

"Let's have a look."

Nighthawk examined it, pulled the trigger several times, rolled the cylinder, and returned it to the
old man.

"Won't do," he said.

"What's the matter with it?"

"Feels stiff."

"Of course it feels stiff. It's metal."

"I meant the mechanism."

"So oil it."

"I'd never trust it," said Nighthawk. "And if I don't
trust it, I'll never use it—so why buy it in the first
place?"

"You feel this way about every new weapon you
buy?"

"I've never owned a new one."

"You owned many?" asked the old man dubiously.

"A few."

"Can I show you anything else?"

Nighthawk looked around, saw a knife with a ser-
rated blade, slipped it comfortably inside his right boot.
"Yeah, I'll take this, too. What's the total?"

The old man totaled up the amount, scanned

Nighthawk's retinagram and thumbprint, waited for the bank's computer to validate them, transferred the money to his store's account, and began to wrap the weapons.

"Don't bother," said Nighthawk. He positioned the Burner's holster on his thigh, waited for it to bond with his trousers, then attached the Screecher's holster to the small of his back. He took the tiny batteries and shoved them into a pocket.

"You know," said the old man, "you look like a man who was used to carrying weapons once upon a time."

"Once upon a time I was."

"You develop a sudden grudge against someone?"

"Maybe someone's got a grudge against me."

"Who'd want to bother a dignified old guy like you?"

"Beats the hell out of me," said Nighthawk, walking toward the door. Suddenly he stopped.

"Hey, old man," he said.

"Yeah?"

"You have to register those weapons, don't you?"

"Yeah, but there's no problem. I know your name: Jefferson Nighthawk."

"Tell you what. Register them to Dr. Gilbert Egan of Deluros VIII, and I'll give you my vehicle. You can pick it up at the spaceport tonight."

"The papers are in it?"

"Right."

The old man grinned. "Dr. Egan, you got yourself a deal."

Nighthawk turned and walked out into the street. He looked around for Kinoshita, couldn't see him, and walked over to the bar. The doors irised, and as he walked in he found himself facing Johnny Trouble.

"Well, look who's here," said the young man in mocking tones.

"I'm just meeting a friend here," said Nighthawk. "I don't want any trouble."

"Looks to me like you came dressed for trouble, old man," said Johnny Trouble, gesturing toward the Burner at Nighthawk's side.

"Look, kid," said Nighthawk, "I've had a bad morning. I don't need any more hassles."

"Then take your Burner out real carefully, drop it on the floor, and buy me a beer, and you won't have any problems." Johnny Trouble flashed a grin at the handful of men who were seated at tables toward the back of the tavern.

"If I've done anything to offend you, I apologize," said Nighthawk. "I'm leaving the planet in another half hour, and you'll never have to see me again."

"Your money's good here. Your apologies aren't."

Nighthawk stared at him. "Back off, kid. I apologized once. I'm not going to do it again."

"Then you're going to wish you had," said Johnny Trouble, stepping closer.

Suddenly Nighthawk's right hand shot out, so fast that it was almost a blur, and slapped Johnny Trouble's face, hard. The young man spun around from the force of the blow. When he had completed the circle and was facing Nighthawk again, he found his nose two inches from the business end of the older man's Burner.

"Who *are* you?" demanded Johnny Trouble.

"You'll find out soon enough," answered Nighthawk. "Now take that pistol out—gently—and place it on the bar."

Johnny Trouble did as he was told.

Nighthawk placed his own pistol on the bar, an equal distance away.

"Okay, big shot," he said. "Are you ready to face down the Widowmaker a second time?"

Johnny Trouble stared into Nighthawk's cold, unblinking eyes, and didn't like what he saw there. He froze for a moment, then managed to shake his head vigorously.

"Then walk away and don't come back."

Johnny Trouble walked stiffly out the door.

There was a long silence. Then one of the men at the back of the tavern spoke up. "You really the Widowmaker?" he asked.

"Don't believe everything you hear," said Nighthawk, picking up his pistol and putting it back in his holster.

"Are you saying you're not?" asked a second man.

"I wouldn't believe *that*, either," said a third.

Nighthawk smiled at them, then walked out into the street. He saw his vehicle parked in front of the bank building that also housed the insurance agency, walked over, and sat in the passenger's seat. Kinoshita came out a moment later, spotted him, and joined him inside the vehicle.

"It'll be about two weeks before the adjusters send in their report," he announced. "They'll deposit the money in your account."

"That'll be fine," said Nighthawk.

"I looked into all the stores," continued Kinoshita. "I didn't see anyone I recognize."

"Then they're gone. No great surprise."

"So where to now?"

Nighthawk pointed at the sky. "Out there somewhere. We'll improvise as we go."

They drove to the spaceport.

"Damn!" exclaimed Kinoshita as they came to a stop. "You know what we forgot to do?"

"What?"

"Sell the vehicle."

"It's been taken care of," said Nighthawk, climbing out.

Kinoshita followed him as they walked through the spaceport and then out to where their ship was sitting.

"Something's wrong," said Nighthawk softly.

"What are you talking about?"

"Never mind. But when I give the word, hit the ground."

Kinoshita looked around, couldn't see any sign of

life, and decided that the older man was being overly cautious. He was about to say so when Nighthawk yelled *"Duck!"*

Kinoshita hit the concrete and heard the hum of Nighthawk's Burner just above his head. There was a scream some thirty yards to his left.

"Okay, you can get up now," said Nighthawk.

"What happened?" asked Kinoshita, standing and brushing himself off. "Who was it?"

"A very foolish young man," said Nighthawk, walking over and turning the body face-up with his boot. There was a smoking hole between its dead, staring eyes.

"Johnny Trouble!" exclaimed Kinoshita.

"I *told* him it was an unlucky name," said Nighthawk, totally devoid of emotion.

You're peeking through again, thought Kinoshita. *You were buried so deep inside that old man, I thought you might never show up. But here you are, as cold and efficient as ever. You may rue the day they burned down your house and brought you back, but this much I know: Someone else is going to rue it even more.*

Chapter 8

♦ ♦ ♦ ♦ ♦ ♦ ♦

⬩⬩

Nighthawk looked at the image of the green world floating
above the navigational computer.

"What do you think?" he asked.

"It's pretty enough, I suppose," replied Kinoshita
noncommittally.

"Ninety-seven percent Earth gravity, breathable
air, plenty of water."

"Has it got a name?"

"Alpha Spinoza IV."

"No," said Kinoshita. "I mean a *name*."

"Pondoro."

"What does it mean?"

"Who knows?" replied Nighthawk.

"What kind of population?"

"Two Tradertowns, nothing else that I can find.
Population is about six hundred permanent residents,
with a daily average of maybe fifteen hundred transients."

"It's not on the major trading routes," said Kinoshita. "Why so many transients?"

"It's a safari world. Half the transients are out hunting, and another quarter are getting ready to go out or preparing their trophies after coming back."

"Are you going to take up big-game hunting?" asked Kinoshita sardonically.

"Not me," answered Nighthawk with a smile. "I've hunted the biggest."

"Then what's the attraction?"

"It's small, it's underpopulated, it's off the main trade routes, and it looks pleasant enough. There'll be a constant stream of supply ships for the Tradertowns and hunting lodges, so we shouldn't have too long to wait for anything we need. And with the very real possibility of a hunter getting ripped apart, I figure there's got to be decent medical care."

"Are you sick?"

"No."

"Well, then?"

"I'm an old man," replied Nighthawk, "and getting sick is what old men do."

"You're only sixty-two."

"I've been sick before, I'll be sick again. Not with the same thing, I hope, but it's inevitable."

"I don't think you're ready to move into a nursing home just yet," said Kinoshita.

"No, but when the time comes, I'll be ready to. I've seen otherwise rational men go a little crazy at the mention of nursing homes, as if they were synonymous with concentration camps."

"Still, it's hard to picture you needing or accepting help from anyone."

"Count on it." Nighthawk paused. "I came very close to dying once. I didn't like it."

"What about all those times you risked your life?" persisted Kinoshita.

"It went with the job . . . and I never risked my life if there was an alternative."

"How many times weren't there alternatives?"

"A few." Nighthawk looked at the pleasant green image again. "Yeah, I think we'll try our luck here."

They broke out of orbit and were soon on the ground. Nighthawk summoned a robot and had it take their luggage to Customs.

"Robots?" said Kinoshita, surprised. "On a world with only six hundred people?"

"They're not for the residents," answered Nighthawk. "They're for the tourists."

They rode the slidewalk to the spaceport's main building, and were soon being interviewed by Customs officials.

"May I have your passport, please?" asked the woman who was processing Nighthawk.

He handed it over. "I'm surprised."

"Oh? About what?"

"I've been on a lot of worlds. You're the first live Customs official I've encountered. Usually it's all computerized and dehumanized."

"We believe in the personal touch on Pondoro."

"It's appreciated."

"Which safari company will be meeting you, Mr. Nighthawk?" she asked.

"None."

"You haven't decided on one yet?"

"I'm not here for a safari."

Suddenly she smiled. "*That's* why we have live officials."

"I beg your pardon?"

"We're here to handle the unexpected," she explained. "You're the first visitor in more than a year who wasn't here to go hunting." She paused. "May I ask what business you have on Pondoro?"

"None."

"If you're just here for service or refueling, you needn't pass through Customs."

"I'm considering buying some property and settling down," said Nighthawk.

She ran his passport through her computer again. "You haven't been to Pondoro before," she said, staring at a screen that he couldn't see.

"I know."

She frowned. "There must be something wrong. It says that you're—"

"I know," interrupted Nighthawk. "A hundred and seventy-four years old."

"Yes."

"I've been in DeepSleep at the Cryonics Institute on Deluros VIII for a hundred and twelve years. You can check it out."

She uttered two short commands to her computer, then looked up.

"Welcome to Pondoro, Mr. Nighthawk. I'm delighted to see that you've made a complete recovery."

"Thank you," replied Nighthawk. "I wonder if I might make a request?"

"Certainly. What can I do for you?"

"You can keep my name to yourself. I'm sure your computer has told you who I am. I'd prefer to leave all that behind me and begin a new life here on Pondoro."

"I won't tell anyone," replied the woman. "But your name is registered in the computer, and it will remain there until you legally change it. At that time, if you'll contact me and show me proof of your new name, I can adjust the computer to reflect that."

"Thank you."

"I never thought I'd meet the Widowmaker," she said. "I saw holos of you when I was a little girl. Most people thought you'd been dead for almost a century even then."

"I wouldn't believe everything I saw if I were you," replied Nighthawk.

"Are you certain you wouldn't like to go on safari, a man like you?" she continued. "I can recommend some of our best companies."

"No, thanks."

"You're sure I can't change your mind?"

"I'm sure."

"Let me try anyway," she said, uttering more commands to her computer.

Suddenly, without moving, Nighthawk found himself in the middle of a forest. Standing some twenty feet away was a red-and-black catlike carnivore, some six hundred pounds, its orange unblinking eyes focused on him as it crept forward.

Nighthawk found to his surprise that he was holding a sonic rifle in his hands.

The carnivore roared once and leaped at him, and Nighthawk, with no time to raise the rifle to his shoulder, fired from the hip, spinning to his left to try to evade the creature—

—which froze in mid-leap. Instantly the forest and the weapon disappeared, and Nighthawk was once again in front of the Customs agent.

"What the hell was *that*?" he demanded.

"Just a sample," she replied. "The real thing is much more exciting."

"If you say so."

"So . . . can I interest you in a safari?"

He shook his head. "I told you what I'm here for."

"I know—but I get a commission for every safari I sell," she said apologetically. "We're a one-industry world."

"Does your industry include a hotel for people who haven't decided what company they want to use?"

"There's only one hotel in town. You'll find it easily enough."

"I thought there were two Tradertowns," said Nighthawk.

"There are. But the other is almost two thousand miles from here, in the southern hemisphere—or the eastern one, depending on which way you look at it."

"Has the hotel got a name?"

"The Pondoro Taylor." She paused. "The hotel, like our world, is named after John Taylor, one of the greatest big-game hunters in human history."

"Never heard of him," answered Nighthawk. "I thought our greatest hunter was Nicobar Lane."

"Taylor lived thousands of years earlier, back when we were still Earthbound."

"So why isn't the world named Taylor? What's Pondoro got to do with it?"

"Pondoro was his African name. I gather it was a native word for lion, and as an indication of his courage it was considered a mark of great respect."

"What's 'African'?"

"A city or country back on Earth, I'm not sure which." She paused. "The hotel supplies a computer in every room. I'm sure you can call the information up from your computer's data banks once you're there."

"Speaking of which, how do I get there?"

"Just pick up your luggage and glide out to the front of the spaceport," she answered. "You'll find some transport vehicles there. Enter whichever one you want and tell it where you want to go."

"Robot driver?"

"No driver at all," she replied. "Or, rather, the vehicle drives itself." She smiled. "Don't look so concerned, Mr. Nighthawk. I know they didn't exist when you entered DeepSleep, but we've only had one accident in the fifty-three years we've been using them."

She handed him back his passport card after her computer had added a Pondoro visa to its coding, and he joined Kinoshita at the front door of the spaceport.

"Very friendly people," said Kinoshita.

"They seem to be."

"Did you get the holo of the charging . . . I don't know what you'd call it—kind of dinosaur?"

"No, I got a cat."

"Amazing how quickly they can put you in the jungle, isn't it?"

"I don't think I was *put* in the jungle so much as surrounded by it," answered Nighthawk.

"Whichever."

They approached the first vehicle in line. The doors slid back to allow them to enter, and the robot accompanying them loaded their luggage.

"Where may I take you?" asked the vehicle.

"The Pondoro Taylor Hotel," answered Nighthawk.

The vehicle immediately sped off down the narrow road leading to the Tradertown.

"Is it any good?" asked Kinoshita.

"Is *what* any good?"

"This hotel."

"I hope so. It's the only one in this hemisphere."

Kinoshita looked out the window. "Pretty country. More savannah than forest, at least around here." A herd of herbivores caught his eye. "Some pretty grass-eaters out there. Nice spiral horns on the males."

"There is no hunting allowed without a license," announced the vehicle.

"We weren't going to hunt," replied Nighthawk.

"Furthermore," continued the vehicle, ignoring his answer, "all areas within ten miles of the spaceport and the Tradertowns are protected reserves, where hunting and fishing are both illegal."

"Fine," said Nighthawk.

"I could supply you with a hard copy of all the safari companies based on Pondoro," offered the vehicle in its toneless voice, "as well as prices for their various services. Some of them will lead holographic as well as hunting safaris."

"That won't be necessary."

"Would you care for a list of all the game animals on Pondoro?" continued the vehicle. "I can produce holographs of each."

"No."

"Please inform me if you change your mind."

"You'll be the first to know," said Nighthawk. He turned to Kinoshita. "I've got a sinking feeling that this might not be as tranquil a world as I'd hoped."

"All the shooting?" suggested Kinoshita.

"All the selling."

They rode in silence and came to the Tradertown in another ten minutes.

"Not exactly typical," commented Nighthawk. "One bar, one casino, one weapon shop, one taxidermist, and twelve safari companies. Usually you've got half a dozen bars, drug dens, and whorehouses for every other building in town."

"We have reached the Pondoro Taylor Hotel," announced the vehicle as it pulled to a stop. "I have registered you for two single rooms. If you prefer to share a room—"

"Single rooms are fine," interrupted Nighthawk.

"My services will be billed to your personal account, Mr. Nighthawk."

"Fine," said Nighthawk. "Let us unload our bags and you can be on your way."

"I will take your luggage to the service entrance, and it will be delivered to your rooms." The vehicle waited for both of them to emerge, then quickly pulled around a corner of the building.

Nighthawk and Kinoshita approached the front desk, where a uniformed man awaited them.

"Welcome to the Taylor," he said. "Your rooms are on the second floor, keyed to your voiceprints. Just tell the doors to open and they'll respond."

"Which doors?" asked Kinoshita.

"The ones with your names on them in holographic displays," answered the man. "Is there anything I can do to make your stay more comfortable?"

"Yeah, there is," said Nighthawk.

"Excellent! I can recommend the very best safari guide, the finest weapon for—"

"All I want is the name of a realtor."

"A realtor?"

"Someone who sells real estate."

The man frowned. "I don't believe we have any, sir."

"What happens when you want to buy a piece of land?"

"I see!" responded the man. "You mean a private hunting preserve!" He paused. "Just ask the computer when you get to your room."

"Thanks," said Nighthawk. "One more thing. Where do we find a good meal?"

"I suppose you could get some sandwiches in the bar across the street," came the answer. "But the Taylor has the only restaurant in town."

"How late is it open?"

"It's open around the clock," answered the man. "You never know what time a ship might land, or when a safari might come in from the bush."

"Thanks," said Nighthawk. "We'll freshen up and unpack, and then come down for dinner."

He walked over to an airlift, followed by Kinoshita, and floated up to the second floor. They walked down the corridor until they came to doors with their names emblazoned, commanded them to open, and entered.

The luggage was already there, and after Nighthawk washed the dust from his hands and face he walked to the desk in the corner and activated the computer.

"How may I help you?" asked the machine.

"I want to relocate to Pondoro," said Nighthawk. "What properties are available?"

"With or without a domicile?"

"With, preferably."

"There are four private hunting lodges for sale, and one timeshare, all within forty miles of this Trader-town. Would you care to see them?"

"Please."

The five domiciles suddenly appeared above the computer. Beneath each was a price and a plat of the land.

"I'd like to see the four lodges tomorrow," said Nighthawk. "Who do I contact?"

"I have just arranged appointments at one-hour intervals beginning at noon," answered the computer. "Any empty vehicle near the hotel will take you there."

"Thank you. If I wish to make a bid, who do I make it *to*?"

"You will make your bid to me, and I will transmit it to the owners."

"Fair enough. Deactivate."

Nighthawk walked out into the hall, decided to wait for Kinoshita in the restaurant, and descended to the main floor.

Kinoshita joined him a few moments later.

"Did you learn anything?"

"There's a few places for sale. We'll visit them tomorrow afternoon."

"That means we get to sleep late?"

"*You* do. *I've* got to find someone who can give me a new ID and passport."

"In a typical Tradertown, I'd say you'd have your choice of forgers," said Kinoshita. "On this world, I'd be surprised if you can find even one."

"Lot of pretty pictures on the walls," commented Nighthawk, gesturing to the paintings and holographs of game animals.

"So what?"

"So any artist who can do that can do what I need. If I can't change my name legally, I'll hire one of them to make up some ID papers for me."

"Got a name chosen yet?"

"I'll think of one before morning."

They ate a meal of alien game meats and exotic produce, and then, because it was a lovely, cool night, they decided to sit outside before going off to bed.

The hotel had a veranda overlooking a small pond. Very few animals came by, but the building and its lights hadn't scared the birds off, and Nighthawk and Kinoshita sat on comfortable chairs, watching them.

"You know," remarked Kinoshita after a few minutes, "maybe there's something to this bird-watching after all."

"Maybe you've found a new hobby."

Three men walked out of the hotel's bar, headed for a table on the veranda. One of them stopped when he was a few feet from Nighthawk and stared at him.

Nighthawk stared back without saying a word.

"Mack! Blitz!" said the man, calling to his companions. "Come over and take a look."

Kinoshita tensed as the two other men joined their companion in front of Nighthawk.

"You got a problem, friend?" asked Nighthawk easily.

"Listen!" said the man. "It's *him*!"

"Boy, he sure as hell looks like him," agreed the one called Blitz. "And like Rimo says, he sounds like him, too."

"But it can't be," said Mack. "Take a *good* look. He's an old man. That was just a kid."

"Anyone can color his hair," said the first man, the one called Rimo. He took a step closer. "You ever been on a world called Tundra?"

"Tundra?" replied Nighthawk. "Never even heard of it."

"Damn it, that's *his* voice!" said Blitz.

"Maybe you remember the Marquis of Queensbury?"

Nighthawk shook his head. "I never heard of *him*, either. You're looking for someone else."

"Come on, guys," said Mack. "We're going out into the bush at daybreak. Let's get some sleep."

"Maybe we've found something to hunt right here," said Rimo doggedly.

"I've got no quarrel with anyone," said Nighthawk. "It's a lovely night out. Why not just enjoy it and go about your business?"

"Look at him!" said Mack. "He's got to be fifty-five, maybe sixty. It can't be the same guy."

"I don't care!" snapped Rimo. "I know who it is!"

Just be quiet and keep still, thought Kinoshita. *They've been drinking. Don't rile them. Any minute now they'll realize you can't be the twenty-three-year-old who killed the Marquis.*

"I've never seen you before in my life," offered Nighthawk.

"That's kind of funny, because *I've* sure as hell seen *you!*" said Rimo.

Don't egg him on. Just be quiet and polite and humble and they'll walk away.

"You must be mistaken," said Nighthawk.

"And *I* think you can't hide who you are behind a gray wig!" shot back Rimo.

Kinoshita sensed a change in his companion, took a quick look at Nighthawk's face, and had a sudden sick feeling in the pit of his stomach—because it wasn't Nighthawk's face anymore. It was the Widowmaker's.

"Son," said Nighthawk, "we've done enough talking, and you're standing in my way."

"You going somewhere?" demanded Rimo pugnaciously.

"No."

"Then what's your problem?"

"I'm watching birds."

"Are you?"

"And fools."

Shut up! You're an old man. They may be a little drunk, but there are three of them, damn it! And they're young.

"Who are you calling a fool?"

"If the shoe fits," replied Nighthawk. "You're looking for a kid. Do I look like one to you?"

"You look like an old man who hasn't got the brains to keep his mouth shut."

"And you look like three corpses."

"Corpses?" Rimo laughed. "We're not dead!"

"You will be soon enough if you don't walk on," said Nighthawk ominously.

"You don't have to do this!" whispered Kinoshita.

"*They* don't have to do this," answered Nighthawk, not lowering his voice. "I was just sitting here minding my own business."

Blitz's hand snaked down toward his laser pistol.

"Don't do it, son," warned Nighthawk.

Blitz's fingers grasped the handle of his gun. Nighthawk's hand flashed as he stood up, and suddenly a knife buried itself in Blitz's neck. Mack went for his gun, but Nighthawk's laser fried him before he could withdraw it.

"Who the hell *are* you?" demanded Rimo, who had been watching, too surprised to move.

"The name is Jefferson Nighthawk." Pause. "Now aren't you sorry you asked?"

"What happened to you?"

"I grew up," said Nighthawk grimly. "And now *I've* happened to *you.*"

"Walk away!" said Kinoshita urgently. "Don't go for your gun and he'll let you live!"

"Fuck you!" snapped Rimo. "I'm going to be the man who killed the Widowmaker!"

He reached for his weapon, Nighthawk's Burner spewed out its deadly light again, and the younger man fell heavily to the ground.

Nighthawk stepped down from the veranda and nudged each body with his toe while his pistol was still trained on it, just in case there was a spark of life left. Finally he turned to Kinoshita. "Who the hell was the Marquis of Queensbury?"

"He was an outlaw, or maybe you'd call him a warlord," answered Kinoshita. "He controlled half a dozen worlds. Word has it that your first clone killed him."

"You never saw him?"

Kinoshita shook his head. "No."

"So along with Hernandez's men, I could run into the Marquis' men all the hell over the Frontier."

"It's possible."

"And of all these hundreds, maybe thousands, of men who have a grudge against the Widowmaker, you can identify five or six?"

"That's right."

"Shit!" muttered Nighthawk angrily. "All I want is to be left alone!"

You may think that's what you want, but you could have kept quiet and eventually they'd have gone away. Jefferson Nighthawk may want to be left alone, but the Widowmaker is growing stronger every day. I didn't think you were ready to take on three men at once, but he knew, didn't he?

"Well," said Nighthawk with a sigh, as the Widowmaker vanished to some secret place inside him, "let's find out who's in charge and report this. It'll look a lot better than if we just wait for them to find the bodies."

"Right," agreed Kinoshita.

We all have our agendas. You've got yours, which is out in the open. I've got mine, which I haven't confided to you. And I have a feeling the Widowmaker has his—and only he knows what it is.

Kinoshita sighed deeply.

I wonder what happens when they clash, as sooner or later they will?

Chapter 9

◆ ◆ ◆ ◆ ◆ ◆ ◆

◈

Nighthawk sat in the mayor's office, which happened to be a wood-paneled den at the Big Seven Safari Company.

"Damn it!" he said softly as he and Kinoshita waited for the mayor. "I'm an old man. My enemies have been dead for a century. I shouldn't have to watch my fucking back!"

"They weren't *your* enemies," said Kinoshita for perhaps the fifth time. "They were your clones'."

"Same goddamned thing!" snapped Nighthawk. "I've earned a little peace and quiet! I spent forty-five years on the Frontier, I went up against every human and alien outlaw I could find, I never ducked a fight, I never asked for favors." He took a deep breath, then released it slowly. "I've *done* my duty, damn it!"

"You could have let them walk away," suggested Kinoshita gently.

"They'd just have come back."

"You don't know that."

"I'm trying to be a man of peace," said Nighthawk irritably. "You know I am. But you can push *any* man just so hard and just so far—*even* a man of peace."

"Couldn't you have held off another ten seconds?" said Kinoshita. "Another fifteen? Maybe they'd have left."

"And if they had, maybe they'd have harassed some other old guy who *isn't* Jefferson Nighthawk."

"And maybe they wouldn't have."

"No more guessing games," said Nighthawk. "They went for their weapons. It was self-defense, and I don't think you're going to see a lot of mourners at their funerals."

A well-built middle-aged man, with shoulder-length silver hair and wearing an outfit made of native animal skins, entered the den, looking almost like a poster for his company. He spotted Nighthawk and walked up to him.

"Mr. Nighthawk?"

"Right," said Nighthawk, shaking his extended hand.

"My name is Hawkeye Silverbuck."

Nighthawk smiled. "It is?"

Silverbuck returned the smile. "It is now. And you must be Mr. Kinoshita."

"I am," replied Kinoshita.

"Pleased to meet you," said Silverbuck. "I am the mayor and chief law officer of Pondoro, as well as the owner of the Big Seven Safari Company." He paused. "Mr. Nighthawk, would you care to tell me exactly what happened in front of the Taylor just after nine o'clock tonight?"

"Three men thought I was someone else and threatened to kill me. When they went for their weapons I was forced to defend myself."

"Were there any witnesses?"

"I saw the whole thing," said Kinoshita. "He's telling the truth."

"Let me amend that," said Silverbuck with a

smile. "Were there any witnesses who could reasonably be considered objective observers?"

"I don't know," said Nighthawk. "But that's the way it happened. And the moment it was over, I came here to report it to you."

"Did you do or say anything to encourage them?" asked Silverbuck.

"I tried to *dis*courage them. Why?"

"You say it was a case of mistaken identity. If you goaded them into a fight and they didn't know who they were facing, I would consider that tantamount to murder. After all, you *are* the Widowmaker."

"I *was* the Widowmaker," Nighthawk corrected him. "Now I'm just an old man looking for a place to live out his life."

"I think the presence of three dead bodies belies that statement," said Silverbuck. "I've checked, and there was paper on two of them." He smiled in amusement. "So now it's up to me to decide whether to pass the reward on to you or charge you for killing them."

"Bullshit," said Nighthawk. "If they were wanted men, how can you charge me with murder?"

"They were wanted for robbery. I know you've been away, but robbery is still not punishable by death."

"Then give me some sodium-P, or hook me up to a Neverlie Machine, and let's get this over with," said Nighthawk.

"I don't think that will be necessary," said Silverbuck. "I'm sure we can settle this quickly and amicably."

"Oh?" asked Nighthawk suspiciously.

"And I'll make sure you receive the reward."

"Not necessary."

"But I insist."

Nighthawk stared at him. "In exchange for what?"

"It's very simple. Leave Pondoro and promise never to come back."

"I didn't break the goddamned law!"

"It doesn't make any difference," replied Silverbuck. "Once word gets out that you're here, every young gun on the Inner Frontier will make a beeline for Pondoro to go up against you." He paused. "We do a lot of killing here, but we prefer to confine it to animals."

"They don't have to know I'm here. I plan to get new ID papers tomorrow."

"If you hadn't killed three men, I could probably keep your identity a secret, but now . . ." Silverbuck let his voice trail off. "It's a lot harder to change a police record than a Customs registration form—and yes, I'm aware than you plan to change it."

"Damn it!" snapped Nighthawk. "You have no legal right to make me leave!"

"I'm the only elected official and the only lawman on this planet, or at least on this half of it. My word carries the full force of the law, and I'm telling you we don't want you here." He paused. "Hell, *you* don't want to be here, either," he continued reasonably. "Go deeper into the Frontier, and establish a new identity *before* you land on the world where you want to live."

"I'm staying," said Nighthawk adamantly.

"I've already explained why it would be foolish to stay," said Silverbuck. "Why are you being so stubborn?"

"The Widow—" he began, and quickly caught himself. "*I* don't run from threats."

"No one's threatening you. I'm just telling you what will happen if you stay."

"You're the law. Your job is to protect me."

"I'm the law by default, Mr. Nighthawk," said Silverbuck. "No one else was willing to accept the position. But I spend most of my time on safari—and to be perfectly honest, I'd be a lot better protecting you from animals than men."

"Some lawman!" snorted Nighthawk contemptuously.

"You want the job?" shot back Silverbuck. "Just say the word and it's yours. Two thousand credits a month, and no one can deport you. Kill anyone you want; see if I give a damn."

"I'm retired."

"I saw what you did in your spare time."

"They went for their weapons."

"We're back where we started. I'm accepting your story, but I want you off the planet tomorrow—or I'll reopen the investigation."

"I'll let you know."

"Think about it very carefully," continued Silverbuck. "You don't want me as an enemy, Mr. Nighthawk. I know better than to go up against you; no one could pay me enough to do that. But I'll hide in a blind, and nail you from a quarter mile away. You'll never know what hit you—and I guarantee that with *my* rifles, I don't miss at four hundred yards."

Suddenly Silverbuck was looking down the barrel of Nighthawk's Burner.

"What makes you think I'll let you get four hundred yards away, Mr. Silverbuck?" asked Nighthawk in low tones.

Silverbuck raised his hands, too frightened to say anything.

"I've been threatened by experts," continued Nighthawk. "I don't rattle."

"You killed a lot of men," Silverbuck said with more confidence than he felt. "But you were always a lawman or a bounty hunter, never an outlaw. You won't kill me."

"I learned a long time ago never to bet more than I could afford to lose," replied Nighthawk. "Are you prepared to bet your life on that?"

Silverbuck shook his head.

Nighthawk lowered his Burner and put it back in its holster. "I'll leave when I'm ready to."

With that, he turned on his heel and walked out of the building. Kinoshita considered apologizing for his behavior, thought better of it, and followed him into the street.

"He's right, you know," said Nighthawk.

"Then why did you pull a gun on him?"

"There's a difference between being right and being arrogant. Telling me how he's going to kill me is arrogant."

"So what do we do now?"

Nighthawk was about to answer when there was a small commotion at the doorway to the tavern.

"*That's him!*" someone shouted.

"*Did you hear what he did?*"

"*Is he really the Widowmaker?*"

"*He's an old man. How could he—?*"

"*—killed all three of them before they could get off a shot.*"

"*Yeah? Well, wait till he goes up against Billy Tuesday!*"

"*I hear Backbreaker Kimani is already on his way here!*"

"Yeah," said Nighthawk disgustedly as he turned and approached the doorway to the Taylor, "it's time to move again."

Chapter 10

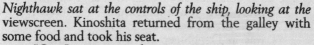

Nighthawk sat at the controls of the ship, looking at the viewscreen. Kinoshita returned from the galley with some food and took his seat.

"Can I get you anything to eat?"

"No."

"Mind if I ask where we're going?"

"Go ahead."

"All right," said Kinoshita. "Where are we going?"

"I don't know."

Kinoshita stared at him for a long moment. "Are you mad at the whole galaxy, or just those members of it who remember the Widowmaker?"

Nighthawk made no reply, and Kinoshita ate his meal in silence.

"You mind if I say something?" he asked after a few more minutes had passed.

"Yes."

"Damn it, Jefferson, just how long are you going to be like this?"

"Until I feel differently."

"I could die of old age before that happens."

"*I'll* die of old age first."

"Not you," said Kinoshita. "You'll die taking on twenty men at once, all the while protesting that you just want to be left alone."

Nighthawk turned to him. "Just what the hell do you expect me to do?"

"The last clone had cosmetic surgery," Kinoshita pointed out. "He's got a new face and a new identity. No one will ever know who he is, or was. If you're so hot to live a peaceful life, why don't you do the same thing?"

"In case it's escaped your attention, I've *been* doing the same thing, and it hasn't helped a bit . . . so why bother? It was a lousy idea to begin with. I'm still Nighthawk; it's the Widowmaker I'm getting rid of. These are my face and my name. They're two of the things that define me. I don't see any reason to change them."

"I could give you four reasons," answered Kinoshita, "but they're all dead."

"I was in DeepSleep for a hundred and twelve years," said Nighthawk angrily. "I shouldn't have to hide who I am. My enemies should all be dead."

"But they're not. You yourself would be dead if we hadn't created two clones to earn enough money to keep you alive until a cure for your disease was found. But in the process, the clones made new enemies, enemies who haven't reverted to dust yet. Now, that's a fact, and all the arguments about what life *should* be like aren't going to change it." Kinoshita paused. "You know, so far we've only mentioned the Marquis and Colonel Hernandez. But the last thing your second clone did was kill Governor Cassius Hill and a few hundred of his best soldiers. He had a standing army of close to four million men and women who had a pretty soft touch until you came along. Probably most of them would like to see you dead, too."

"I assume you've got a point?" said Nighthawk dryly.

"Yes, I do. I think the odds are no worse than even that you're going to run into someone who has a grudge against the Widowmaker, or someone's who's out to make a reputation for himself, on just about every inhabited world on the Inner Frontier. If you think otherwise, you're blinding yourself to the facts. You need a new name *and* a new face."

"Forget it."

"But you yourself were going to get a new ID back on Pondoro!"

"I've given it a lot of thought the past few days." Nighthawk placed a finger to his cheek. "I spent five years looking for some trace of this face in the mirror. All I could find was some kid's nightmare. Now that it's back, it's staying."

"That's stupid!"

"That's me."

"The hell it is. Your clones were always willing to adapt to conditions. Why the hell aren't you?"

"My clones were young men with their whole lives ahead of them. I'm an old man, and most of my choices have been made, for better or worse. I'm through adapting to conditions; from now on, they can adapt to me."

"So you're going to keep killing men on each new world we come to?"

"I hope not. It's up to the men."

"It doesn't have to be."

"We're talking about *my* choices, not yours," said Nighthawk. "Why are you having such a problem with that?"

"You're good," said Kinoshita. "Even at sixty-two, you're far better than I was in my prime. You know, I seriously wondered if you had a chance against those three guys back on Pondoro, but you were never in any danger, were you?"

"Not really."

"I know," continued Kinoshita. "But you know something? As good as you are, I've seen better. And younger."

"Who?"

"Your clones. Either of them could take you out in a heartbeat."

"So what? One's dead, and the other's vanished with a new name and face."

"You're not following me," said Kinoshita. "If *they* could take you, probably there are others who could, too. You won't know and I won't know until you go up against one of them. I'd rather see you avoid it and live the life you keep saying you *want* to live."

"I *do* want to live it." Nighthawk's jaw muscles tightened noticeably as he grimaced. "I tried to walk away from that kid on Churchill, just as I tried to let those men on Pondoro walk away from me."

"So why didn't you?"

Nighthawk sighed deeply. "Because I've been the Widowmaker too long."

"You're not going to change, you know."

"I know."

"And someday, sooner or later, as you get slower and weaker, and the young men who want to challenge you get faster and stronger, one of them's going to kill you."

"At least it'll be quick," said Nighthawk with no sense of regret or resentment. "I've had my fill of the slow way."

"Wouldn't you rather never again be in a situation where you have to kill or be killed?" asked Kinoshita.

"If I've really got four or five million enemies out there, I'm just as likely to be backshot as called out."

"That's better somehow?" demanded Kinoshita sarcastically.

"Look," said Nighthawk. "I appreciate your concern. I hope you're wrong. I suspect that you're right. But this is the face I've lived with, and it's the one I'm going to die with."

"All right," said Kinoshita bitterly. "Get yourself killed. See if I care."

"You *do* care. What I can't figure out is why."

Kinoshita was about to reply when the ship's computer interrupted them.

"We are being followed by a Class J spacecraft," it announced.

"How long has it been on our tail?" asked Nighthawk.

"Twenty standard minutes. After fifteen minutes I attempted to elude it, as per your programming, but my evasive maneuvering was unsuccessful. I am a 341 Golden Streak; it is a 702 Bullet, which means that it is faster than I am."

"Find its port of origin and get its registration," ordered Nighthawk.

The computer was silent for a moment, and then spoke again: "Owned by the Starburst Corporation, seventeen hours out of Pondoro."

"How long since *we* left Pondoro?"

"Nineteen hours."

"Where are Starburst's corporate headquarters?"

"Tundra."

Nighthawk looked over at Kinoshita. "Not much question about it, is there?"

"None."

"Can you put it on the viewscreen?" asked Nighthawk.

"I can put a representation of a generic 702 Bullet on the screen. This particular ship is still out of range."

"If it's been chasing us since Pondoro, how come you only noticed it twenty minutes ago?"

"I do not know that it has been chasing us since it left Pondoro. It came within range of my sensors twenty-one minutes ago. I only know what it has done since then."

"Well," mused Nighthawk, "we can't outrun it, and there's no sense leading it to a planet we might want to settle on. I suppose the best thing to do is to talk to it."

"Make sure the damned thing isn't armed first," suggested Kinoshita.

"No Class J craft carries armaments," said the ship.

"Send it a greeting," ordered Nighthawk.

"Sending . . . done."

"Put any reply on visual and audio."

The holograph of a burly man suddenly appeared in front of Nighthawk and Kinoshita.

"Hello, Nighthawk," said the man with a toothy grin. "Tired of running?"

"No one's running."

"Are you going to tell me you didn't try to lose me about five minutes ago?"

"Automatic programming," answered Nighthawk. "I didn't even know you were there."

"Well, you know it now, and you'll know it when you land."

"Why are you following me?"

"You killed three of my friends."

"I never saw any of them before."

"Sure—and you don't know who I am, either." The man laughed in amusement.

"That's true."

"You disappoint me," said the man.

"Oh?"

"You were a lot of things back on Tundra, but you were never a liar. And now you've lied to me three times in less than a minute."

"I haven't lied at all."

"You said you didn't try to lose me, you said you didn't know the three men you murdered, and you said you didn't recognize me. Any way you count it, that comes to three."

"I killed those men in self-defense," said Nighthawk. "Don't make me do the same to you."

"Oh, I know better than to take you on alone," said the man. "After all, you're the Widowmaker—or at least that's what they say. But you're going to pay for killing my friends." He paused. "If it'll make you feel any better, I didn't mind your killing the Marquis. I never liked him much."

"I can't tell you how relieved that makes me feel," said Nighthawk dryly.

The man laughed again—a loud humorless laugh. "You want to tell me where your next port of call is, or are we going to have to do this the hard way?"

"The hard way, I think," said Nighthawk. "Computer, cut the transmission."

The holograph vanished instantly.

"What are we going to do?" asked Kinoshita. "We're not fast enough to lose him."

"I know."

"So what's next?" persisted Kinoshita. "I suppose we could try to lead him back to an Oligarchy world and—"

"I don't let the Oligarchy do my fighting for me," said Nighthawk.

"Then where *do* you plan to go?"

"Well, there's no sense blowing another habitable world by leading him to it."

"It sounds like he's got friends with him," offered Kinoshita.

"That's *their* problem," responded Nighthawk. "Mine is finding the best place to face him."

"You have something in mind?"

"Yeah, I think so. I've been in this section of the Frontier a couple of times before." He paused. "Computer, how far are we from Bolingbroke VI? In hours, not miles or parsecs."

"At this speed, encountering no ion storms, I can reach the Bolingbroke system in thirteen hours and twenty-seven minutes."

"Do it."

"Programming . . . done."

"Good, I'm going to grab something to eat."

Nighthawk walked off to the galley, and Kinoshita began questioning the computer about the Bolingbroke system.

"There are eleven planets, including four gas giants, and two asteroid belts. The seven inner planets possess atmospheres."

"How many oxygen worlds?"

"None."

"None?" exclaimed Kinoshita, surprised. "Then what is Bolingbroke VI?"

"It is a methane world, mean temperature minus seventy-three degrees Celsuis."

And that's where you want to face this guy and his henchmen? If they don't kill you, the planet will.

Chapter 11

◆ ◆ ◆ ◆ ◆ ◆ ◆ ◆

Bolingbroke VI looked like it had been put together from a billion twinkling stars. Exquisite crystalline growths reached toward the distant sun, acting as prisms for its light. The ground was rough and uneven, as if covered by an infinite number of glass shards, each reflecting a different color.

"It looks like a big piece of rock candy," remarked Kinoshita.

"I suppose it does," said Nighthawk, testing all the joints of his protective suit.

"So what's the big attraction about facing them on Bolingbroke?"

"I like it here."

"That's *it*?" demanded Kinoshita. "You're standing out in the open on a frozen methane planet, ready to face God knows how many men, just because you like it here?"

Nighthawk smiled in amusement. "You never spoke like that to my clones, did you?"

"They wouldn't have permitted it," admitted Kinoshita.

"Lucky for you us old men are more tolerant, isn't it?" said Nighthawk, still smiling.

"Damn it!" said Kinoshita in frustration. "Can't you even tell me why we're here? I can help!"

"I don't need your help," replied Nighthawk. "I told you that when we landed. You'll be much safer if you just go back to the ship."

"Not a chance."

"Why?" asked Nighthawk. "Not only don't I need you, but you don't owe me a thing."

"I'm staying right here."

"You didn't answer me."

"*You* didn't answer *me*, either," shot back Kinoshita.

Nighthawk stared at him for a moment, then shrugged. "What the hell, you're a grown man. Suit yourself."

"I still don't know why you chose to face them on an airless planet."

"Bolingbroke's not airless," Nighthawk corrected him. "It has an atmosphere."

"Nothing anyone I know can breathe."

"That's not what I said."

"Okay, it's not airless. Big deal."

"It's important," said Nighthawk.

Kinoshita frowned. "If you say so . . . but I sure as hell can't see why."

"Hopefully, neither can *they*," said Nighthawk, pointing to the sleek silver ship that was plunging down toward the planet's surface.

Kinoshita looked up. "They'll be on the ground in another three minutes."

"Give or take," agreed Nighthawk.

"And you plan to just stand here in the open and wait for them?"

"That's right."

"If they land over there," continued Kinoshita, pointing to his left, "they can hide behind those outcroppings and shoot you down at their leisure."

"I imagine that's just what they'll try to do," agreed Nighthawk.

"Damn it! I'm supposed to be your partner! Why can't you tell me what the hell you have in mind?"

"I don't have any partners," replied Nighthawk firmly. "I appreciate your friendship and your loyalty, but I told you to stay in the ship. It's *your* decision to stand beside me, not mine."

"Will you please stop sounding like the goddamned Widowmaker and go back to being Jefferson Nighthawk?"

Nighthawk stared at him, but said nothing.

"Look, I'm sorry," said Kinoshita awkwardly. "I didn't mean that."

"Yes you did, and there's no need to apologize. I've never held it against a man for saying what he felt. Honesty is an underrated virtue these days."

Kinoshita shifted his weight awkwardly. "Just the same, I'm sorry."

"Fine."

"Let me know what you want me to do, and I'll do it. This is your show."

"You don't have to do anything. I thought I already told you that."

Kinoshita looked down at Nighthawk's hands. "Shit!" he exclaimed.

"What is it?"

"You wore the wrong gloves. Those are the metal-plated ones for working on the ship's engine. You'll have a hard time holding a pistol."

"I'll manage."

"I could go back right now and . . . No, of course you can't change them out here. Your hands would freeze. You'd better go to the ship and change while you can."

"There's no time," said Nighthawk, pointing to the

pursuing ship, which had just touched down and was disgorging a handful of armed men.

"Six, seven, eight," counted Kinoshita. "*Eight!* Do you really think you can take eight men at once? I mean, maybe when you were thirty-eight, but now . . . ?"

"If I have to."

"If you have to? What does that mean?"

"It means I hope I don't have to," said Nighthawk calmly, as he turned to face his pursuers.

The largest of the eight men stopped by a glittering outcropping of purplish crystal. "You picked a hell of a planet to die on, Widowmaker," he said.

Nighthawk and Kinoshita picked up his radio signal with almost no static, and the former answered into his helmet's transmitter: "Then don't kill me."

The man threw back his head and laughed heartily. "You've got a wonderful sense of humor! I don't remember your having any back on Tundra. Five years bumming around the galaxy has done wonders for you."

"I don't suppose you'd like to tell me who you are, and why you're here?"

"Are you kidding?" demanded the man.

"I just want to know what name to put on your grave," came the answer. Kinoshita noted that even the tenor of the older man's voice had changed. Nighthawk had totally vanished; it was the Widowmaker speaking now.

The man gestured with his hand, and his seven cohorts instantly spread out, always keeping outcrops between themselves and Nighthawk.

"You got any short prayers, Widowmaker? I don't think you've got time for a long one."

"You're sure you want to go through with this?"

"Am *I* sure?" The man laughed again. "You got balls, Widowmaker; I'll give you that. But I've got eight guns, and we're well protected. You're two old men out in the open. What are you going to do now?"

"Applaud your superior generalship, I suppose," said Nighthawk.

He held his hands out so they could see he wasn't holding any weapons, then clapped them together once.

As metal plate struck metal plate, it was as if a bomb had exploded. At the sound of Nighthawk's hands striking each other, every outcrop within a quarter mile collapsed like so much broken glass, burying the men standing beside or behind them.

"Shoot this in the air," said Nighthawk, pulling a small bullet gun out of a hidden pouch on his thigh and handing it to Kinoshita. As Kinoshita began firing it every few seconds, creating ear-shattering explosion after explosion, Nighthawk withdrew his Burner and put a lethal burst of solid, silent light into each of the eight men as they struggled to dig themselves out from beneath the crystal shards.

"Jesus!" muttered Kinoshita, looking at the carnage. "Jesus!"

"You look upset," noted Nighthawk calmly as he walked back and rejoined him.

"I keep forgetting who you are," said Kinoshita. "It was like a walk in the park for you! Sixty-two years old, and you wiped out eight men without drawing a deep breath!"

"Would you be less impressed if I were thirty-two years old?" asked Nighthawk dryly.

"How the hell did you know it would work on an airless world?"

"I told you: it has an atmosphere. No air, no molecules. No molecules, no way for sound to travel."

"And that's why you wore the metal-plated gloves?"

"I knew they'd make a noise, and I couldn't be sure I could fire the pistol before they shot me down."

"You also had to know they'd stand next to the outcroppings," added Kinoshita.

"Well, I figured that between my reputation and a display of confidence, they'd make sure they had some cover before the shooting started. And by standing in the open, where they could see me if I made any sudden moves, it encouraged them to take cover before they pulled their weapons."

"It's just *business* to you, isn't it?"

Nighthawk shook his head. "It used to be my business. It isn't anymore."

"Sometimes you can't hide from who you are."

"I'm Jefferson Nighthawk."

"And the Widowmaker."

"That's not who I am. It's who I *was*."

Something in the tone of his voice convinced Kinoshita not to continue the discussion. Instead he walked over to the eight corpses, turning a few over with the toe of his boot, studying their faces.

"That's quite a haul," he said at last.

"There are no more men than there were five minutes ago," responded Nighthawk, unimpressed.

"That's not what I mean. I recognize three of these faces. I've seen them on Wanted posters. I'll bet there were prices on the others, too."

"Good," said Nighthawk. "It means I won't have to answer a charge of murder if they're ever found."

"Found?" asked Kinoshita, puzzled.

"Right. Let's get to work. We've got time to bury them before nightfall."

"Are you crazy? I'll bet the lot of them are worth more than half a million credits. Let's pack 'em in the cargo hold and take them to the nearest bounty station."

"Not interested."

"You're running through money pretty quickly," said Kinoshita. "Here's a chance to add to your bankroll. Legitimately."

"I said no."

"Why not?"

"Because I'm not the Widowmaker anymore. I'm retired. I don't kill men for bounties."

"You're crazy!" snapped Kinoshita. "They're already dead! What's wrong with hauling them to a bounty station?"

"Nothing's wrong with it," answered Nighthawk. "I'm just not going to do it."

"What *do* you plan to do for money?"

"If I need it, I'll work for it."

"And *this* wasn't work?" demanded Kinoshita.

"A century ago it was work. Today it was survival, nothing more."

"What *is* work?" persisted Kinoshita. "You're no farmer. You're no artist. You don't know shit about investing. You're too old to do heavy labor. If you're not going to claim these bounties, maybe you'd better consider becoming a marksman in a carnival like that Billybuck Dancer."

Nighthawk stared at him silently for a long moment, until Kinoshita shifted uncomfortably. Finally he spoke.

"These men were fools. I'd never chase someone onto a world of his own choosing. And having come here, they were even bigger fools for facing me. There's no price on my head, no reward for killing you. If they wanted to kill us, all they had to do was blow our ship away and then leave. We'd have no food, almost no oxygen, and no way of radioing for help."

"Son of a bitch!" exclaimed Kinoshita. "I never thought of that!"

"Neither did they," said Nighthawk, making no attempt to keep the contempt from his voice. "But just because *they* were fools, it doesn't mean all the men out here are fools. The Frontier is a hard place, and it breeds hard men and women. Most of the fools die young, and I don't plan to spend the rest of my life facing what's left. I told you: I spent enough time in death's company that I cherish the years that remain to me. The Widowmaker's retired. For good."

"But this is a different case," said Kinoshita. "No one's asking you to go out after the Oligarchy's Most Wanted list. These men are already dead, and there just happens to be paper on them. Why can't we just pack them in the hold and turn them in? You may never have had to worry about money before, but you do now. This ship cost a bundle, and you'll never recoup your loss on Churchill II, and . . ."

"I said no."

"But—"

"Why did they come after me?" asked Nighthawk.

"Because you killed three of their friends."

"And why did those three come after me?"

"Because your first clone killed the Marquis of Queensbury."

"So I killed one man, and three came after me. Then I killed those three, and eight more came after me. It's a fucking geometrical progression. I'm sure each them has half a dozen friends who will want my blood once they find out that I killed them . . . so it stops here. We bury them, we leave the planet, and no one ever knows what happened here." He paused. "And if no one knows, no one forces me to kill them. Otherwise, one of these days I'll have to go up against one I can't kill."

"All right," said Kinoshita. "I see your point."

"Then let's get to work."

Nighthawk burned eight graves in the ground with his laser. Then he and Kinoshita rolled the bodies into them and covered them with tons of crystal shards. Finally, because he was a thorough man, he blew away every outcropping within a mile of the graves, so no one could chance upon the one spot where the natural cover had been upset.

And, hopeful that he could finally live the life of tranquility he so coveted, Jefferson Nighthawk took off from Bolingbroke VI and sped deeper into the Inner Frontier.

Chapter 12

◆ ◆ ◆ ◆ ◆ ◆ ◆ ◆

◈

Nighthawk had been in a black mood since leaving the Bolingbroke system, and Kinoshita had given him as wide a berth as possible within the cramped confines of the ship.

They passed several inhabited worlds. Each time Nighthawk would find some reason not to set the ship down, and they sped farther and farther away from populated areas of the Inner Frontier.

Finally Kinoshita could take the silence no longer.

"Are you ever going to speak again?" he demanded, rotating his chair to face Nighthawk, who was sitting motionless in the captain's chair.

"I'm speaking right now."

"You know what I mean."

"I've got nothing to say," replied Nighthawk, staring without interest at one of the viewscreens at the front of the small cabin.

"Bolingbroke's nine days behind us and you haven't

said ten words since we left," complained Kinoshita bitterly. "I'm going stir-crazy!"

"If you're unhappy, I'll drop you off anywhere you want," said Nighthawk.

"I don't want to be dropped off!" snapped Kinoshita. "I just need to hear a human voice."

"You're hearing it right now. Happy?"

"What the hell's the matter with you, Jefferson? We hid all the bodies on Bolingbroke. There's no chance that anyone's going to find them in this lifetime, probably not ever. No one's coming after you. You've got your health. So what's got you so pissed off?"

Nighthawk finally turned to face him. "I would think it'd be obvious," he said.

"Not to me."

"Look," said Nighthawk. "I went into the deep freeze for a hundred and twelve years. I'd become a monster, and I lived in pain every day for close to a decade before they put me under. I awoke to a universe where everything had changed, where every single person I knew had been dead for decades. But I told myself that I had one advantage: I wouldn't have the problems that usually accrue to retired men in my profession. There'd be no young guns out to build their reputations, no old guns with scores to settle. They were all dead, and I could spend my final years in some semblance of peace and tranquility."

He paused, and Kinoshita could see the bitterness on his face as well as hear it in his voice. "So what happens? I find out that not only *don't* I have that advantage, but I don't even know the men who want to kill me, or why they're after me."

"We *had* to create those clones to pay for your upkeep. You know that."

"Damn it, Ito—I didn't have to go into the fucking cryonics lab! I'm not afraid to die; a hundred and twelve years ago death would have come as a welcome relief. I submitted myself to the freezing process because I weighed all the possibilities, and I could see myself enjoying a comfortable, tranquil old age once they developed a cure. If I'd known that I was going to be hunted by men I never saw before . . ." He shrugged. "I think I might have endured the pain for one more month a century ago and gotten it over with."

"Don't even think that!" said Kinoshita firmly. "If you'd died, there would be a hell of a lot more evil abroad in the galaxy today."

Nighthawk stared curiously at him. "I don't know what you're talking about."

"Your clones did what they had to do, what they were created for," answered Kinoshita. "They went out and killed the bad guys—and for every enemy they made, they earned the gratitude of hundreds more."

"That's comforting in a detached, academic way," replied Nighthawk. "But no one's shooting at my clones."

"There are tens of thousands of oxygen worlds on the Frontier. I'm sure we can find one where nobody knows you, where no one's ever even heard of the Widowmaker."

"Didn't someone quote me some very discouraging odds about that not too long ago?" asked Nighthawk with an ironic smile.

"What do you want me to say?"

"Nothing," came the reply. "It was you who wanted *me* to talk, remember?"

"All right," said Kinoshita, leaning back in his chair and rotating it from one side to another. "We'll talk about something else."

"Fine."

"So how did you become, well, what you are, in the first place?"

"What I am is an old man, and I got here by outliving my friends and my enemies."

"You know what I mean," said Kinoshita doggedly. "I became a lawman because I saw my parents shot down in our own house by a thief who panicked when they stumbled upon him. How did you become the Widowmaker?"

Nighthawk shrugged. "I had a talent for killing people."

"What kind of answer is that?" demanded Kinoshita. "How did you know you had this talent? When did you develop it? According to the history books, you were already the Widowmaker when you were eighteen. How old were you when you killed your first man?"

"I was very young."

"How young?"

"Very." Kinoshita shot a quick look at Nighthawk, who seemed more disinterested in giving answers than uncomfortable about them.

"Whom did you kill?"

"Someone who deserved it." Nighthawk paused. "I don't think I've ever killed anyone who didn't deserve it. At least, once upon a time I thought that . . . but I suppose I could be wrong. Age tends to make you second-guess yourself."

"Who was the toughest killer you ever went up against?" continued Kinoshita.

"They were *all* tough."

"I mean—"

"I know what you mean," interrupted Nighthawk. "You want me to name one notorious outlaw, a Santiago or a Conrad Bland. Well, I can't."

"Why not?"

"Think of it this way: Just about everyone on the Frontier carries some kind of weapon, don't they?"

"Yes."

"Have you ever seen a dead man walking around with one?"

Kinoshita frowned. "Of course not. I don't know what you're getting at."

"What I'm trying to say is that every man you see walking around with a weapon in his holster is undefeated in mortal combat . . . and if there's paper on him, you know he's been a participant at least once. Reputations mean nothing. You have to treat each and every one of them as if they're the toughest opponent you'll ever face."

"You're a cautious man," remarked Kinoshita.

"That's how you stay alive out here."

"Your second clone was like that, too."

"Why shouldn't he have been?" replied Nighthawk. "After all, he was me."

"The first clone didn't possess that sense of caution."

"From everything I've been given to understand, the first clone was cannon fodder. They created him with no memories and sent him off on his mission."

"It was the best they could do at the time—and he did accomplish that mission."

"They should have waited until they found a way to give him my memories, the way you did with the second one."

"If they'd waited another two months, you'd have been awakened and evicted while you still had eplasia," answered Kinoshita.

"Still, it was murder, sending him out with no experience, no memory, nothing but some physical skills."

"They were *your* skills."

"There's a difference," said Nighthawk. "*I* developed them to survive in my environment. They became a part of me, and I used them intelligently. This poor clone may have had my gifts, but he couldn't possibly have had my instincts. *That's* why it was murder."

"The second clone thought so, too," said Kinoshita. "That's why he killed Colonel Hernandez."

"He saved me the trouble," said Nighthawk. "Or the pleasure."

"I thought you didn't take any pleasure from killing people," observed Kinoshita.

"Usually. But I think I'd take an enormous pleasure in avenging Jefferson Nighthawk."

"You make it sound like Colonel Hernandez killed *you*."

"He did. A version of me, anyway."

"Both of the clones seemed to feel an almost mystical bond with you," said Kinoshita. "Do you feel it, too?"

Nighthawk shook his head. "I'm the original. I don't owe either of them anything, except a vote of thanks for earning enough money to keep me alive. *They* owe *me* everything, including their existence."

"You know, you can be a cold son of a bitch sometimes."

"We can always go back to not talking."

"Not if you want me to stay sane, we can't."

"As you wish," said Nighthawk, getting to his feet. "But first I'm going to get a beer."

He walked to the galley, put in his order, waited a few seconds for the mechanism to respond, and made his way back to the pilot's chair.

"Next ship we buy knows how to chill its glasses," said Nighthawk, taking a long swallow of the beer.

"*Are* we buying another ship?"

"Depends on whether those guys back on Bolingbroke got off any messages to their friends," answered Nighthawk. "That's why I'm heading toward the Core on a straight line. It should make it easier to spot anyone who's chasing us."

"After nine days I think we're safe," offered Kinoshita. *What a damned silly thing to say. We're safe? Hell, whoever's not chasing the Widowmaker is the one who's safe.*

"Probably."

"And you've passed some interesting worlds the last couple of days."

"One world's pretty much like another."

"I disagree. There was a beautiful one on the outskirts of that last star cluster."

"I don't care if it's beautiful," interrupted Nighthawk. "I care if it's peaceful."

It may be peaceful now, but it won't be once you land on it. You attract trouble the way honey attracts flies.

"What exactly *are* you looking for?" asked Kinoshita. "Do you still want to grow flowers and watch birds?"

"I don't know," responded Nighthawk. "What I mostly want is to be left alone."

"I don't think it's your nature to be left alone." *And I have a feeling that it's not the galaxy's nature to leave you alone.*

"Well, like I told you once before, I'd like a wife, someone to grow old along with me." Kinoshita seemed about to say something and Nighthawk held up his hand. "Someone who doesn't look like you," he added with a smile.

"What happens to me when you find her?"

"What do you think should happen?"

"I'm not leaving you," said Kinoshita adamantly.

"Maybe not, but you're sure as hell sleeping at the other end of the house."

"I don't know if you're joking or not."

"About sleeping at the other end?" repeated Nighthawk. "Absolutely not."

"I mean about my staying."

"I don't know why you want to."

"I have my reasons."

"You plan to share them with me someday?" asked Nighthawk.

"Someday," promised Kinoshita.

Chapter 13

◆ ◆ ◆ ◆ ◆ ◆ ◆

◈

The world was called Tumbleweed. It was the only habitable planet within ten star systems, which gave it more traffic than such a nondescript world would ordinarily receive. There was a refueling station, a shipping depot, an assay office for mining claims in all the neighboring systems, a postal forwarding station for the worlds deeper into the Frontier, a single small city that had evolved from a Tradertown, a huge freshwater sea, and a few enormous totally-automated farms operated by robots laboring under the watchful eye of a tiny handful of human overseers.

"I've got a good feeling about this one," said Nighthawk as they stepped out of the ship.

"I hope you're right," said Kinoshita. "I'm tired of traveling."

"Nobody forced you to."

"I know."

"Well, let's get over to Customs."

Customs was nothing but a machine that registered their passports and added molecular long-term visas to them. Then they were transferred to a bullet-shaped transparent shuttle that glided inches above the ground and took them to the center of the small city.

"Lots of people here, compared to some of the worlds we've seen," remarked Nighthawk.

"Just the same, I'd hardly call it a megalopolis," answered Kinoshita.

"No, but it could mean property costs a little more." Nighthawk paused and turned to Kinoshita. "You've been keeping track of our finances. Where do we stand?"

Kinoshita pulled out a pocket computer and queried it, then looked up. "You've got a little less than two million credits," he announced. "As far as I can tell, the insurance money on Churchill hasn't come through yet, though it could just be slow registering in your account."

"Only two million?"

Kinoshita smiled in amusement. "What's so only about two million credits?"

"How much cash did you bring back with you from Pericles?"

"About five million. But the moment I entered the Oligarchy, it was subject to taxes . . . so it really came to just under three million."

"I'm a little confused," said Nighthawk. "The clones were created because the interest on my principal wasn't enough to pay the cryonics lab, right?"

"That's correct."

"But that was *interest*, and you made it up with the money you brought back. What happened to the principal? There must have been six or seven million credits' worth."

"The interest kept you frozen," answered Kinoshita. "The principal paid for the cure and the cosmetic surgery and your rehabilitation. In fact, it didn't quite pay for it; I had to add some of the Pericles money to it."

"Okay, that sounds reasonable enough," said Nighthawk with a shrug. "I was just wondering."

"It's your money. You have a right to ask."

"We have reached the city limits," announced the shuttle. "I require an address."

"I don't have an address," said Nighthawk. "Take us to the best hotel."

"I do not know which is the best hotel," answered the shuttle.

"Okay, take us to the most expensive hotel."

The shuttle immediately turned left, then right, and soon pulled up to a small hotel.

"Welcome to the Sand Castle," said the robot doorman, coming forward to take their luggage.

"I don't see any sand," remarked Nighthawk.

"This entire section of the city is built on a sand dune," explained the robot. "Hence the name of the hotel."

"I don't see any castle, either, but let it pass."

The robot, which had not been asked a question nor given an order, froze, trying to interpret what Nighthawk had said. Kinoshita stepped forward and directed it to take them to the hotel's registration desk.

Another robot greeted them and, after registering their voiceprints and retinas and matching their credit ratings to their thumbprints, assigned them a pair of rooms on the second floor.

"Have our baggage taken up to our rooms," said Nighthawk. "I want to grab some dinner. Where's your restaurant?"

"I regret to inform you that the Sand Castle's restaurant does not open until seven o'clock local time."

"Where's the closest open restaurant?"

"I am not programmed to send residents to our competition," replied the robot.

"Are you programmed to make value judgments?" asked Nighthawk.

"Yes, in certain instances."

Nighthawk pulled out a pistol. "All right, let's put that programming to the test."

"I must inform you that I have no sense of self-preservation and thus will not respond to threats to my person," said the robot.

"Shut up and listen," said Nighthawk. "If you don't tell me where I can find the closest restaurant, I'm going to blow out the two plate-glass windows in your lobby. I want you to compute their cost, compare it to the cost of losing my patronage for a single meal, and then make a decision."

"The closest restaurant is the Tumbleweed Roadhouse, one hundred thirty-seven feet to the south of this building, sir," said the robot instantly.

"I knew I could count on you," said Nighthawk, holstering his weapon. He turned to Kinoshita. "Let's go."

"What if he reports you to the law?" asked Kinoshita as they walked out the door and turned south.

"Do you know anyone who ever got arrested for threatening to shoot a window?"

"No," admitted Kinoshita with a smile. "No, I must admit I don't." He paused. "What would you have done if the robot hadn't answered?"

"Nothing. No sense shooting the place up if his programming wouldn't let him answer me."

They reached the Tumbleweed Roadhouse, an unprepossessing restaurant, and soon seated themselves at a table. A small, wiry blonde woman approached them.

"What'll it be, gentlemen?" she asked.

"A couple of beers and a menu," answered Nighthawk.

"Don't need a menu. We've got steak, and we've got stew. Take your choice."

"That's not much of a selection."

"My cook quit, my waiter's got the day off, and I don't believe in robots."

"So who did the cooking?" asked Kinoshita.

"I did. And it's a damned sight better than you'll get at the Sand Castle."

"What makes you think we're from the Sand Castle?"

"It's the only place in town that's too snobbish to serve dinner at dinnertime," she replied.

"You've got a point," said Nighthawk.

"So what'll you have?"

"You choose."

"You look like a steak-and-potato man to me."

"I've been a soya man for half a century. Time I started to get used to real meat again."

"Hey!" yelled a young man, dressed in colorful silks and satins and sporting an impressive array of weapons, from a nearby table where he sat with three of his friends. "Enough jabbering! We want some service."

"If you don't like it, complain to the owner," said the woman.

"Fine. Where is he?"

She turned to him and put her hands on her hips. "You're looking at her."

"You don't want to get me mad, lady," said the young man. "Just come over and take our orders."

"I'm taking this gentleman's order," she said. "And no one tells me what to do in my own place. If you don't like the service, there's the door."

"Go take care of them," said Nighthawk. "I don't want to cause any trouble."

"You're not causing any," she replied. "*They* are." She raised her voice. "And the more they cause, the longer they can wait. What's the point in owning your own place if you can't tell anyone to go to hell?"

"Goddammit, Sarah!" said another of the young men.

"You know what happened the last time you hassled me," she said ominously. "You want more of the same?"

"Come on, Sarah," he said defensively. "We just want some food."

"Then you can damned well wait your turn. You know I'm shorthanded."

"What the hell did you do to him?" asked Kinoshita curiously. "The last time he hassled you, I mean?"

"I broke a chair over his head," she answered. "*Nobody* gives me orders in my own place. Two steaks, right?"

"Right," said Nighthawk.

"Don't you worry," she said to Kinoshita. "If he gets uppity, I'll protect you." She glanced at Nighthawk. "You don't look like you need any protecting."

She went off to wait on the other table, and returned with the steaks about ten minutes later.

"Hope you like 'em rare," she said.

"Rare'll do," answered Nighthawk.

"You here on business?"

"Nope."

"Just passing through?"

Nighthawk shrugged. "I don't know. We're looking for someplace to settle down."

She looked from Nighthawk to Kinoshita, then back again. "You two . . . ah . . . ?"

"Just friends."

"Well, if I can show you around, just ask."

"I thought you were all alone here."

"Look around," she said. "When those four would-be Widowmakers finish, you're all that's left."

"Widowmakers?" asked Nighthawk.

"Just an expression. There hasn't been a Widowmaker in more than a century."

"Well, as long as we're all the customers you've got, why not have a seat and a beer?" suggested Nighthawk. "My treat."

"I'll take the seat," she said, sitting down at the

table. "But I'll take a rain check on the beer until the place is closed." She extended a hand. "I'm Sarah Jenner."

"Jefferson Nighthawk. And this is Ito Kinoshita."

"Nighthawk, Nighthawk," she repeated thoughtfully. "Seems I've heard that name before."

"I've never been here before."

"I've only been here five years myself. Hell, I don't think we've got two hundred natives on the whole world. If you grew up somewhere else, Tumbleweed looks idyllic; but if you grew up here, you can't wait to see the rest of the galaxy."

"Where are you from originally?"

"Pollux IV," she said. "Inner Frontier born and bred. I grew up on a farm out there."

"What brought you to Tumbleweed and what keeps you here?" asked Nighthawk. "As long as we're thinking of settling here, we ought to know what its virtues are."

"It's empty and it's clean," answered Sarah Jenner. "That's what got me here. And inertia keeps me here."

"Nothing else?"

"I've got a son," said Sarah. "It seemed like a nice place to raise him."

"If you're shorthanded, why not ask him to fill in here?"

"He's half the galaxy away, on Aristotle."

"The university planet?"

Sarah nodded. "It took every credit I had, but it's been worth it." She paused. "It's lonely without him. Still, I keep busy. I've got my business, and my reading, and my birds."

"You raise birds?" asked Kinoshita.

"I watch them."

"So does he."

She looked at Nighthawk with renewed interest. "You're a birder?"

"Not really. But I think I could become one."

"Hell, I'll take you out tomorrow morning," she

said. "I know some wonderful places for watching."
Suddenly she stopped. "That is, if you're interested."

"Why not?" said Nighthawk.

"I thought we were looking for property," said
Kinoshita.

"Nothing wrong with property that's got birds on
it," replied Nighthawk.

"I like you, Jefferson Nighthawk," she said. "You
don't find many men out here who like birding."

"I like you, too," said Nighthawk. "You don't find
many people anywhere who like to read."

"I *knew* it!" she said happily. "You're a reader, too!"
She paused. "Tell me you're not a lawman before I get
too fond of you."

"Why?"

"Because if you're here to apply for the job, it's
only fair to tell you that you've got a life expectancy of
less than two weeks."

"Oh?"

Sarah nodded. "That's another reason I sent my
son away. Tumbleweed is a beautiful little world, but
lately it's become a drug drop. They smuggle alphanella
seeds from ten or twelve secret farms to the Oligarchy,
and this is one of the drop points. The last couple of
lawmen we had tried to stop the trade. They were
damned good men." She pointed through a window.
"They're buried about half a mile in that direction. So
before I get too fond of you, I want to make sure you're
not here for the job. I know they've been advertising it
all across the Inner Frontier."

"I'm an old man. Why would I want to be a
lawman?"

"You're not that old," she replied. "And you've got
that look about you."

"What look?"

"I don't know. A look that says it wouldn't be a
good idea to have you as an enemy."

"I just want to be left alone."

"Well, if you don't chew alphanella seeds or wear

a badge, there's no reason why anyone should bother you," said Sarah. "Just don't stand too close to me if any strangers show up."

"Why not?"

"I'm on their hit list."

"The drug runners?"

She nodded. "Tumbleweed used to be a decent place to live. I want it to be again. So I reported them to the Oligarchy. They set up a sting operation on Raleigh II, and killed about ten of them . . . but one of the survivors found out that I was the informer, and since then there've been attempts on my life."

"And you're still here?"

"I'm harder to kill than you might think," she said, her expression a cross between pride and arrogance.

"Well, if you go around hitting young gunmen over the heads with chairs, I can believe it."

"It sounds like this world needs a protector," offered Kinoshita.

"At least one," agreed Sarah.

"I wonder where it can find one," continued Kinoshita.

"Beats the hell out of me," said Nighthawk, totally expressionless. "I just hope when he gets here, he protects me, too."

Sarah stared at him. "I said it before: You don't strike me as a man who needs protection."

"Sooner or later everyone needs it," said Nighthawk.

"Hey, Sarah, can we get some coffee?" asked the young man at the other table.

She stared at him impassively.

"Please," he added hastily.

"Happy to," she said, getting up and vanishing into the kitchen.

"Well?" asked Kinoshita.

"Well what?"

"Do you want me to spell it out?"

"I'm too old to go back to being a lawman. This place can find some other savior."

"And *her?*"

"I like her. She's bright and she's tough." He paused. "I think we'll stay in town a few days so I can keep an eye on her. Just in case."

"But you won't take the job?"

"I gave up the hero business a century ago."

"Sure you did."

"I did," repeated Nighthawk decisively.

You're fighting a losing battle, thought Kinoshita. *You can deny it all you want, but you can't help being the Widowmaker. That's why you're going to stay in town . . . and in a curious way, that's why I'm going to stay, too.*

Chapter 14

• • • • • • • •

"*Got one,*" *said Nighthawk.*

"Where?" asked Sarah, following him down the winding path between the tall trees and aiming her lens in the direction he was pointing.

"Top branch. Silver, almost phosphorescent. See how she shines when the sun hits her?"

"Yes, I see her now. She's gorgeous!" She lowered her lens and turned to him. "And you can see her with your naked eye? That's amazing!"

"I've always had pretty good eyesight."

"That's not just good—it's exceptional. Especially for a man in his fifties."

"Older than that."

"Oh?" she said. "How old are you, Jefferson?"

Nighthawk smiled ironically. "Well, there's some debate about that."

"It sounds like there's a story there."

"Someday I'll tell it to you." He looked back into the tree. "So what do you call that bird?"

"Officially, it's not a bird at all."

"It's not?"

"They only have birds on Earth. It's an avian—a flying animal. But it looks like a bird, and it acts like a bird, so I call it a bird."

"Makes sense to me. What kind of bird?"

"Almost none of them have been named yet," replied Sarah. "Avianology isn't one of Tumbleweed's more popular pastimes." She paused. "I guess that gives you the right to name her anything you want."

"I think I'll call her a Silver Sarah."

"I'm flattered." Suddenly, she smiled. "You know, if I were to let my hair grow out, it would almost be that color."

"Why don't you?"

"Being blonde makes me feel young."

"Is that important?"

"Don't *you* ever wish you were young again?"

He shook his head. "I'll settle for being old and alive. The graveyards are full of men who were young and foolish."

"I'll wager you put a lot of them there yourself," said Sarah.

"Why should you say that?"

"Just a guess." She shrugged and shifted the box lunch from one hand to the other. "Probably I'm wrong. I think I know most of the famous killers, good and bad, on the Frontier, but I've never seen you before. Your name rings a bell, but I can't quite place it."

"Don't blame yourself," replied Nighthawk. "You're a century too late."

"I don't understand."

"A hundred and twelve years ago I lay down to take a nap. I just woke up a few months back."

She stared at him curiously. "You were frozen?"

"Yes."

Her eyes widened. "On Deluros?"

He nodded.

"Oh, Jesus—you're *him*!"

"Probably."

"You're the Widowmaker! You're really him!" she continued excitedly. "I'd heard rumors, legends, that you'd contracted some horrible disease and had yourself frozen until it was cured, but no one ever knew any details. I *knew* you had that look about you! I knew it!" Suddenly she laughed and shook her head. "Here I am, babbling like a schoolgirl. I'm sorry."

"You're not afraid to be with the Widowmaker?"

"You always fought for the good guys," she replied.

"Sometimes I did bad things on their behalf," he pointed out.

"Necessary things. You were the best lawman and bounty hunter who ever lived."

"That was a long time ago. Before you were born. Hell, before your great-grandparents were born. Now I'm just an old man who wants to learn birding and catch up on my reading."

"You can tell me the truth, Jefferson," she said. "I'm on *your* side. Your here for the drug runners, aren't you?"

He shook his head. "I'm here for me."

"Really?"

"Really," replied Nighthawk. "Why did you inform on them in the first place? They'd surely have left you alone if you'd kept quiet."

"My son had a drug problem. He chewed alphanella. It almost killed him. When I found out where he was getting the seed, I blew the whistle." She stared at him. "I'd do it again."

"You must have known they'd come after you."

"I was hoping the Oligarchy's sting would nail them all," said Sarah. "But I'm prepared to live with the consequences of my actions."

"That's more than most people are prepared to do," noted Nighthawk.

"That's their problem."

"How many drug runners are there?"

"Who knows? Five, ten, twenty. They recruit killers of every shape and size from all over the Frontier." She smiled wryly. "A real equal-opportunity employer."

"Maybe the Widowmaker can lend a hand."

"It's not necessary," she replied. "You're not here for them, and I'm not afraid of them."

"I admire your courage," said Nighthawk. "But it does you no credit. Nobody in his right mind faces odds of twenty-to-one."

"*You* did."

Nighthawk smiled. "There are plenty of men who would swear that I was never in my right mind." The smile vanished. "Besides, it was my job. It's not yours."

"This is my home. I'm not running away."

"I'm not suggesting that you do," said Nighthawk. "I just think that you could use a little help."

"I appreciate your offer, but the answer is no," said Sarah adamantly. "I'm the one they want; I'm the one who has to cope with the situation."

"Whatever you say." Nighthawk walked along the path, searching for more birds. "There's a bright red one at ten o'clock."

"I know what you're thinking."

"I'm thinking that if you keep talking, you're going to frighten it away."

"You're thinking that you'll pretend to agree with me, but when the drug runners show up, you'll protect me."

"I'm too old to protect anyone." Nighthawk looked to his right. "Purple-and-gold one at three o'clock."

"I remember hearing legends about you when I was a girl," continued Sarah. "You were one of my heroes. You never walked away from a fight in your life."

"I ducked one for a hundred and twelve years."

"But when you were ready, you won."

Nighthawk looked uneasy. "*I* didn't win. The doctors did. And it took a pair of younger Widowmakers to pay them."

"I don't understand."

"I'm not totally sure I do, either," he replied. "Are you getting hungry? We could have lunch."

She stood in the trail in front of him, staring into his eyes. "Why *are* you here?"

"Just chance."

"I don't believe in chance."

"I didn't believe a healthy man could contract eplasia. Fat lot of good it did me."

"What was it like?"

"Pretty bad."

"I've heard of it, of course, but I've never seen anyone with it."

"Consider yourself lucky," said Nighthawk.

"I take it you don't want to talk about it?"

"I don't even want to think about it. Children dream of things that look half as bad and wake up screaming."

She set the basket down, pulled out a blanket, spread it on the ground, and sat down. Nighthawk joined her a moment later, and she passed him a sandwich and a container of beer, then served herself.

"What did you mean about two younger Widowmakers?"

"When I entered the cryonics lab, I left a fortune with my attorneys. They were to invest it conservatively and pay for my upkeep with the interest." He smiled wryly. "That's before Nadine Kirogi became Governor of Deluros VIII and started applying her theories to the economy. The result was twenty-three percent inflation for six years, and suddenly the interest wasn't enough to cover my expenses."

"What happened?" asked Sarah. "They obviously didn't throw you out in the street."

"What happened was that an offer came in for the Widowmaker's services. I was incapable of going out to the Frontier—hell, I was incapable of even standing up—but they decided to create a clone and send *him* out."

"I thought that was illegal."

"When did a little thing like legality bother doctors or lawyers?"

"So the clone went out and did what he was supposed to do?" she asked.

"I think so."

"You *think* so?"

"He was very young and very naive. He never made it back, and the man he was working for swore he didn't fulfill his contract." Nighthawk paused. "Of course, the man he was working for also killed him, so I tend to discount his statements. But the fact remains that the clone only earned half the money he was promised—the remainder was due upon completion of the job—and two years later I was in the same situation again. This time they managed to create a clone that possessed not only my skills but also my memories. I gather that caused him some difficulty—the memories were a century out of date—but he accomplished his mission, and that's why I'm here."

"Where is he now?"

Nighthawk shrugged. "Out on the Rim with a new name and a new face, according to Kinoshita."

"What has Kinoshita got to do with all this?"

"He trained the first clone."

"And the second?"

"The second didn't need any training, but Kinoshita traveled with him. He knew if he ever came back to Deluros they'd terminate him—after all, they'd broken half a dozen laws just by creating him—so he sent Kinoshita back with the money that kept me alive while he established a new identity."

"And you've never met him?"

"Never."

"Aren't you curious?"

"Not really. I know what I was like when I was forty-one, which is what he'd be now."

"But to see a perfect replica of yourself . . ."

"He's not a perfect replica anymore. And if he wanted to see me, he'd find me. I'm not hiding from anyone." He paused. "He did his job. He's under no further obligation to me or anyone else. I think if I were him—and in a way, I am—I'd have no desire to see the original, either. It's almost like coming face-to-face with your God, or your creator."

"That second clone—was he the one who caused all the ruckus on Pericles IV?"

"Yes."

"I should have known that nothing short of the Widowmaker could have pulled that off!"

"How could you know?" said Nighthawk. "The Widowmaker vanished a century ago."

"The Widowmaker is more than you, Jefferson," she explained. "It's you, and your clones, and your legend. You're more alive today that you ever were."

"Then maybe you should consider letting the Widowmaker help you."

Sarah shook her head. "For your own good, I can't let you do it."

"Don't worry about me," replied Nighthawk, totally without bravado. "Over the years a lot of men have tried to kill me. I'm still here."

"That's not it," she said.

"Then what's the problem? I like you, and I want to help you."

"You have no official standing here. And the Oligarchy's sting nailed all the known members of the gang. To the best of my knowledge, none of the men or aliens who are still at large have prices on their heads." She paused. "Don't you see? If you kill them, you're breaking the law. It seems ridiculous on the face of it, but you could conceivably be arrested for murder."

"We can sort it out later," answered Nighthawk. "If worse comes to worst, I'll just leave Tumbleweed and go further toward the Core."

"No," she said firmly. "I can't let you do it on my behalf."

"And that's the only reason?"

She stared at him silently for a long moment. "There could be as many as twenty of them."

"And you plan to face them alone?"

"Of course not," she responded. "But I plan to protect myself. This is my world; I know where to hide, how to set traps. What would *you* do?"

"I'd wait for them at the spaceport and explain they weren't wanted here."

"And when they laughed in your face?"

"Not many people laugh at me," said Nighthawk.

"You'd just stand there and face all twenty of them?" she said. "All by yourself?"

"Why don't you leave that to me?"

"Because I like you, too, and I don't want you getting killed on my behalf."

"I don't plan to get killed. I've spent too much time and energy and money staying alive."

"I appreciate your offer, Jefferson," she said, "but it's not your fight."

"We'll discuss it later," said Nighthawk, opening up his cannister of beer.

"Let's discuss it now," she insisted. "You have no legal right to kill any of them. If you face them and lose, you're dead; if you face them and somehow manage to win, you're a felon. I won't be responsible for that."

"All right," he said. "We'll do it your way."

"Thank you."

A long pause.

"Why are you looking at me like that?" he asked.

"You're a man who's gotten his way all his life," she replied. "You gave in too easily."

He smiled. "Try to be a more gracious winner."

"When I'm convinced I *have* won."

"No problem. I've never been an outlaw; I don't plan to start now."

They finished their meal in silence.

"You must have seen a lot of worlds," she said as they got to their feet and began following the trail again.

"A few."

"Tell me about them."

"There's not much to tell. I was always there on business. You start watching birds, you forget to watch for bullets and laser beams." He shrugged. "Besides, it's been over a century. Most of them will have changed beyond recognition by now."

"It seems sad to have been so many places and not to have any memories of them."

"Oh, I have memories. But not of the worlds; just what happened on them."

"Didn't you ever just want to relax?"

"I've been relaxing for the past hundred and twelve years," he replied. "It's an easy habit to get into. Now I'd like to relax for the rest of my life."

"So you really came here to settle down?"

"It seems remote. That's what I need."

"Why?"

"The less people, the less enemies."

"All your enemies should have been dead for fifty or sixty years," she said.

"You'd think so, wouldn't you?" he said with a trace of bitterness.

"What am I missing?"

"My clones managed to get a few thousand very dangerous people pissed at them." He paused. "At least I knew what *my* enemies looked like. These guys come out of nowhere, and I've never seen any of them before."

"The clones' enemies really come after you?"

"I'm the Widowmaker," said Nighthawk. "That's all they have to know."

"How long have you been out of the cryonics lab?"

"Maybe four or five months. Then I spent some time in the hospital, getting cosmetic surgery and regaining my strength, so I haven't been on my own too long—but it was long enough for them to burn down my house on Churchill, and I had to kill some of them on Pondoro, and more on Bolingbroke."

"And you didn't know any of them?"

"Not a one."

"Well, some deity with a sense of humor is getting even with you for giving children nightmares. You're living a nightmare yourself."

"At least I'm still living it," said Nighthawk. He ran a hand through his thick shock of gray hair. "Anyway, that's why I wanted a remote, sparsely populated little world like Tumbleweed. On a place like this I can see them coming."

"Perhaps," agreed Sarah. "But still, that's no way for anyone to live."

"Says the woman who's waiting for a gang of drug runners to come looking for her."

"I'll hide from them and set traps for them and whatever happens, that will be the end of it."

"If there's one thing I've learned, it's that that's *never* the end of it."

"Those bastards turned my son into a seed chewer. I informed on them, and I'd do it again." She set her jaw. "I did what I had to do. I'll take what comes."

"Well," said Nighthawk with a shrug, "If I can't talk you out of it, I can't talk you out of it." He started off down the dirt path. "Let's go find some birds."

They spent the next hour walking through the forest, spotting an occasional bird, exchanging an occasional reminiscence, just relaxing and enjoying each other's company. Nighthawk found himself attracted to her. It certainly wasn't her looks: he'd never been attracted to small, wiry women or to blondes. Probably it was her self-assurance and independence, two traits he admired wherever he found them.

Finally they came to the end of the path and found themselves back at her vehicle, which she had driven to the edge of the forest.

"Shall we go back to town?" she suggested.

"Might as well," replied Nighthawk. "I've got something to do there."

"Hunt for real estate?"

"Not just yet. I think I'll stay in town for a few days and get the feel of the place."

"I think that's a good idea. This isn't exactly a flourishing market. Any property that's for sale today will be for sale next week and next month . . . and probably even next year."

"Good."

"Then, if I'm not being too nosy," she continued, "what's your business?"

"Oh, mostly just paperwork. Where do I go to apply for citizenship?"

"We've only got one government building," she said. "It houses the mayor, the tax collector, the sheriff, the fire department, the building inspector, everything. Probably even the army, if we ever have one."

"Then that's where I want to go."

"It's on the next block," she said as they reached the outskirts of the city and turned onto the main street. "I'll drop you there."

"Fine."

"Would you care to join me for dinner when you're through?"

"Very much," said Nighthawk, as the vehicle came to a stop. "I'll come by as soon as I'm done here. It won't take long."

She left him at the door to the building, drove back to the restaurant, oversaw the changing of the shifts, and was just completing an order for the following week's supplies when Nighthawk walked in.

There was something different about his appearance. It took her about two seconds to spot what it was.

"What the hell is *that*?" she demanded, pointing to the glowing golden badge on his tunic.

He smiled wryly. "Well, I thought as long as I was going to stay here, I ought to be gainfully employed."

Chapter 15

Nighthawk spent an idyllic two weeks. He slept late, ate three hot meals a day, spent most of his time with Sarah Jenner, and his sole duties as a lawman consisted of arresting one unprotesting drunk.

"Maybe they won't come after all," said Kinoshita, sitting in a comfortable wooden chair opposite Nighthawk's desk one evening after dinner. "I mean, hell, there are millions of worlds. If they were smart, they'd open up two dozen new channels. No sense being predictable, not in their business."

"They'll come to Tumbleweed," said Nighthawk with absolute certainty.

"What makes you so sure? Like I said, there are hundreds of possible routes."

"Sarah's here, and they want her."

"You sure she's not just being hysterical?" asked Kinoshita.

"Does she strike you as the hysterical type?"

"No," admitted Kinoshita. "No, she doesn't." He paused. "You're getting fond of her, aren't you?"

"Is there some law against it?"

"No, of course not. But I hear talk that she's got a kid off at college somewhere who had some drug problems."

"I didn't say I was fond of the kid."

"I would think he comes with the mother."

"He's on Aristotle," replied Nighthawk. "It's not as if I have to help raise him. Besides, he may never come back. And if he does, he'll have a degree, which I suspect is more than you or I ever had."

"I'm not trying to interfere," said Kinoshita. "I just worry about you."

"I know. What I don't know is *why*." Nighthawk stared at him. "I keep thinking you're getting me confused with my clone. You've only known me since I woke up. You may think I'm him, but I'm not."

"I like you."

"That's a pretty lame answer," said Nighthawk. "One of these days I'm going to insist on the truth." He paused. "In the meantime, check with the spaceport and see what ships are due in tonight."

"It's two miles away!" protested Kinoshita.

"I didn't say to walk there. There's half a dozen communication devices in the office. Take your choice."

While Kinoshita was raising the spaceport, Nighthawk walked back to the cells to see if his prisoner needed some coffee, but the man was sleeping it off, and he chose not to wake him. He turned and walked quietly back to the office.

"I think they're on the way," announced Kinoshita.

"Explain."

"There's a ship of Darbeenan registry due to land in an hour. But according to its manifest, it's traveling practically empty, and it's only thirty-eight Standard hours out of Quixote."

"So?"

"They grow alphanella in the jungles of Quixote.

And there are all kinds of servicing and refueling facilities there. Why should an empty ship that just took off land here less than two days later?"

"Okay, it makes sense."

"What are you going to do?"

"Whatever I do, I think I'd better do it at the spaceport. Except for you, no one else in this building looks capable of defending himself against the kind of men who figure to be on that ship."

"I'll come with you," said Kinoshita.

Nighthawk shook his head. "You'll stay with Sarah. If they get past me, I want you there."

"You're sure? If I stand with you, there's a lot less chance of them getting past us to Sarah."

"Just do what I say."

Kinoshita sighed. "All right."

"Thanks. I don't want her alerted, so just go on over, order a beer, and if she asks about me tell her I went to bed early. I'm an old man; she'll buy it."

Kinoshita got up and left, and Nighthawk went back to the cells, unlocked the door to the only occupied one, shook his inebriated prisoner awake, and told him to go home. He didn't think he'd be needing the space, but he knew there was a chance that he wouldn't survive the night and he saw no reason to let the drunk go without food and water until someone remembered he was there.

Then he went to check his armory. He searched through it until he found what he wanted, closed up his office, walked out to the official vehicle the planet had provided for him, and drove to the spaceport. He felt he had at least an hour to prepare for his visitors, and he made good use of it.

When the ship landed, he was the only living being on the grounds. He'd sent the skeleton staff home, and stood waiting as the entire crew of the ship— nine men and five aliens—approached the Customs building. They were a mean-looking bunch, all heavily armed.

When they were about thirty yards away, Night-hawk stepped out of the shadows.

"That's far enough," he said.

"Who the hell are you?" demanded one of the men.

"The law."

The man laughed. "You mean they went out and found themselves another sheriff?"

"Actually, my badge says I'm the Commissioner of Police," replied Nighthawk.

"What's the difference?"

"Not much. I'm still the law. And the law says that you have to state your business."

"You go to hell!" snapped the man.

"Then you'd better turn around and go back to your ship," said Nighthawk. "You're not welcome on Tumbleweed, now or any time in the future."

"Do you know who you're talking to, old man?"

"Yeah. I'm talking to a bunch of drug runners who are about to leave the planet."

"We're not here after you. Let us pass."

"Not a chance."

"You got a death wish?" demanded the man. "Look around you. There are fourteen of us."

"That's okay," said Nighthawk. "We've got a big graveyard."

The man looked at him unbelievingly. "Who the hell *are* you, old man?"

"I've had a lot of names," answered Nighthawk. "The one that stuck is the Widowmaker."

"You're *him*? I heard rumors that you were back!"

"For once, the rumors were right."

The man stared at him. "Even the Widowmaker can't take fourteen of us."

"There was a time when I could," answered Night-hawk. "These days I play it safe."

"What do you mean?" asked the man, looking into the shadows.

"Enough talk," said Nighthawk. "Go back to your ship." He paused. "Your weapons stay here."

The man never took his eyes from Nighthawk. "We're not here for you, Widowmaker. We have business with someone else. Let us by and we'll let you live."

"I don't make deals," answered Nighthawk. "Your weapons—now."

The man drew his laser pistol. Nighthawk was faster, and he fired at the man's feet, detonating a small explosive device that was all but invisible in the dim lighting. Four men and two aliens screamed in agony as the force of the explosion blew them twenty feet into the air. Nighthawk hit the other two devices he had planted, and suddenly there was only one remaining man, a teenager who had stood, motionless and transfixed, as the explosions decimated his companions.

Nighthawk stared at him, and put his burner away.

"All right, son," he said. "It's up to you. You can walk away, or you can go for your weapon. There are no more surprises, no more bombs. It's just you and me. Do you think you're up to facing the Widowmaker?"

The teenager stared nervously at him for a long moment, then shook his head.

"Then walk away, and don't let me ever see your face on Tumbleweed again."

"Where'll I go? What will I tell them?"

"I don't much care where you go, and you can tell your bosses that Tumbleweed is off-limits from now on."

"They'll come back for you."

"Like I said, we've got a big graveyard. There's room for everybody."

The teenager backed up a couple of steps, then hesitated and finally stopped.

"I can't go back and tell them that everyone else was killed," he said plaintively. "They'll never believe me. They'll think I sold them out!"

"That's not my problem," said Nighthawk.

"I can't do it!" yelled the teenager.

"Don't be a fool, son."

"No choice!" he wailed. "No choice!"

He reached for his weapon, and was dead before his fingers touched it.

"Stupid!" muttered Nighthawk, walking over and putting another blast into his body, just to be on the safe side. "Just stupid."

He walked to the drug runners' ship, pulled out yet another explosive, placed it into the exhaust vent, and detonated it. Then he walked to a hatch and opened it.

"If there's anyone inside, come out with your hands behind your head. I'm only going to ask you once."

There was no response.

A younger Nighthawk would have thought nothing of entering the strange, darkened ship and seeking out any enemies. The older Nighthawk simply closed the hatch and melted the lock with his laser pistol, leaving the ship sealed and disabled. If there was anyone aboard it, they'd be more than willing to listen to reason in three or four days.

He stopped at the security control room, canceled the red alert he had ordered and left word about the ship, then drove his vehicle into town, leaving it at his office and walking to the restaurant.

Kinoshita immediately got to his feet.

"It's over already?"

"Yeah, it's over," said Nighthawk, walking over to an empty table and sitting down.

Sarah came out of the kitchen.

"I thought you were asleep," she said.

"I will be soon. I had a little business to attend to first." He took his badge off and tossed it onto the table. "I won't be needing this anymore."

"What happened?" she demanded.

"They won't be bothering you anymore."

"Jesus!" she exclaimed, her eyes widening. "You killed them *all*?"

"They didn't give me much choice."

"Much choice? There must have been a whole gang of them! How did you do it?"

"In the safest way possible."

"Is that all you're going to say about it?" continued Sarah.

"Give me some coffee and a piece of pie, and I'll give you the sordid details."

"Why didn't you tell me they were coming?" she insisted. "It was *me* they were after! I could have helped!"

He stared at her without replying.

"All right, all right," she said with a sigh. "You're the Widowmaker. You didn't need any help." She paused. "But you knew you were going to face a whole gang of them. You should at least have taken Ito with you."

"He was where I wanted him."

"Protecting me?"

"There was no guarantee I could stop them."

"If *you* couldn't, how could *he*?"

"You'd be surprised what good men can do under pressure," answered Nighthawk. "And he's a good man."

"How many of them did you kill?"

"Fourteen."

"*Fourteen?*"

"It was legal. I had the badge, and it was self-defense. I even set up a holo camera to record it, just in case I'm ever challenged about it."

"Now, *that's* a holo I'd like to see!"

"It's digitized and locked under my seal in the spaceport's security computer. I'll pull it out if I need it in court. But I don't think I will."

"Damn it, Jefferson, you're just shrugging it off like it was all in a day's work. You could have been killed!"

"That *is* my work," answered Nighthawk. "Or at least it used to be."

"But you did it for me."

"I just figured I was better equipped to handle the situation than you were."

"I've had one man I care for die on me. I don't want it happening again."

"Your kid's father?"

"Yes."

"He was gunned down?"

"No," replied Sarah. "He was a decent, hardworking man, and I loved him. We never married, but we lived together for fourteen years." She paused. "He didn't die heroically. He contracted some disease that could have been cured in two weeks if we'd lived in the Oligarchy, but he hated the Oligarchy and wouldn't leave the Frontier even to save his own life. So I watched him die, bit by bit, and I'd swore I'd never watch someone I love die again."

"I spent a hundred and twelve years and tens of millions of credits *not* to die like that," said Nighthawk.

"There are other ways to die, even when you're the Widowmaker."

"One of them is hunger," he said, forcing a smile. "I'm still waiting for that coffee and pie."

She left without a word and returned from the kitchen a moment later.

"What do you do now?" she asked.

"Eat the pie, drink the coffee, and go to bed. It's been a long day and I'm an old man."

"Stop saying that!" she snapped. "Old men don't do what you did!"

"All right," he said. "I'm in a state of advanced middle age."

"Damn it, Jefferson! I'm trying to get a straight answer out of you. Are you staying or leaving?"

"On Tumbleweed? I'm staying."

"Alone?"

"I hope not. That depends on you."

"My house is a couple of miles out of town. Tell Ito to cancel your room at the hotel."

He stared at her for a long moment. She wasn't the idealized woman he had dreamed about; on the other hand, he had a feeling that a sixty-two-year-old eplasia victim who made a living by killing people wasn't her idealized man. He found her interesting, and comfortable to be with, and attractive enough to think of taking her to bed, and at this point, 174 years into his solitary life, that was enough.

"Sounds good to me," said Nighthawk.

Chapter 16

"What are you doing up?" asked Sarah, turning suddenly at the kitchen counter.

Nighthawk entered the room, wrapping a robe around himself. "I heard you tiptoeing around, so I thought I'd see if you were okay."

"Of course I am. I just wanted a cup of tea. I'm sorry; I didn't want to disturb you."

"It wasn't your fault," he assured her. "I've always been a light sleeper. It probably saved my life a dozen times. I don't imagine I'm about to change."

"Well, can I make you something to eat or drink, now that you're up?"

"Coffee will be fine," he said, sitting down at the kitchen table.

"Cream or sugar?"

"Black. And hot."

"I have some that's imported from Alphard," said Sarah. "Or do you prefer the local brand? I like it better."

Nighthawk shrugged. "Makes no difference," he said. "Coffee's coffee."

"Local, then. No sense wasting money."

"You don't have to worry about money anymore. I'm a rich man, relatively speaking."

"I'm willing to share. I'm not willing to be kept."

"I'm willing to share, too," said Nighthawk. "And one of the things I've got to share is money. I don't mind sharing your food and your house and your bed; I don't expect you to mind sharing my money."

"I'll share it when I need it. But I've always been frugal. I see no reason to change just because I'm living with the Widowmaker."

"You're living with Jefferson Nighthawk."

"Isn't it the same thing?"

"The Widowmaker's retired."

"I thought he showed up at the spaceport last night," said Sarah.

"That was his farewell appearance."

"Can I ask you a question?"

"Go ahead."

"Why?"

"Why what?"

"Why are you packing the Widowmaker away in mothballs?"

"Because I've been putting my life on the line since I was fifteen, and I'd like to stop."

"And do what?" asked Sarah. "Just how many birds can you watch?"

"More than you think," answered Nighthawk. "And I've got the better part of a lifetime's reading to catch up on. And I can do half a thousand other things I never had time to do when I was the Widowmaker."

Sarah shook her head. "Not you."

"Why not?"

"Look," she began, "I *wish* you could learn to relax, and grow old gracefully, but it's not you. You wake up the second you hear me tiptoeing two rooms away. You face fourteen gunmen at the spaceport and kill them all. You see things with your naked eye that I can barely see with my lens at full magnification." She paused and stared at him. "Like it or not, you're the Widowmaker. It's what you do, it's what you are, and I don't think you can hide from it."

"I wasn't the Widowmaker back on Churchill. I was enjoying my life until they burned my house down."

"How long were you there? A year?"

No answer.

"A month?"

Silence.

"Not even a month," said Sarah. "And you wound up killing Johnny Trouble—oh, I know all about it; Ito told me—and Johnny Trouble wasn't even responsible for the fire." She paused again. "Why don't you just admit that you're the best at what you do, maybe the best there ever was, and stop running away from who you are?"

"I'm an—"

"Don't give me that 'I'm an old man' crap again!" she said sharply. "You certainly didn't act like an old man in bed tonight."

"That's not the same thing."

She poured his coffee into a cup and handed it to him. "Could an old man have held off fourteen killers?"

"I planted explosives around the area before they showed up," answered Nighthawk. "I didn't have to shoot fourteen of them; I just had to hit a couple of bombs they didn't know were there. And when I killed those men back on Bolingbroke, I lured them into a situation where all I had to do was make a loud noise and they were buried under shattered crystal."

"Don't you realize what you're saying?" persisted Sarah. "You're even better now, because you use your brain as well as your physical gifts. You're like an athlete who may have lost a step, but makes up for it with added experience."

Nighthawk sipped his coffee thoughtfully. "I

appreciate what you're saying," he replied at last. "But sooner or later every athlete knows it's time to hang it up. There's at least one man out there somewhere who could take me without working up a sweat—my second clone. And if there's one, why shouldn't there be more?"

"I'm not suggesting you go out looking for them," answered Sarah. "But I think you'll go stir-crazy if you do nothing but read and watch birds and sit around the house. Tumbleweed needs a police officer. Not much happens here, and I'm sure the drug runners won't come back, not after the way you decimated them— but there should be enough going on so you won't be bored to death. And there's one more thing."

"What?"

"Even if there are a few men out there who can take you, they're not likely to show up on Tumble-weed." She smiled. "You're not coming in to clean up some hellhole like you used to do all over the Inner Frontier a century ago; you'll just be keeping the peace on a tranquil little world where nothing too exciting ever happens."

"It happened tonight."

"That was an aberration."

"Most killings are."

"Are you going to consider what I said," said Sarah heatedly, "or are you going to spend what's left of the night arguing with me?"

"I'll give it some thought," said Nighthawk. "But there's one thing that you haven't taken into account."

"I don't want to hear any more age crap."

"No more age crap."

"Then what?"

"I'm tired of killing."

"*Can* someone like you be tired of killing?" she asked dubiously.

"Especially someone like me," he assured her. "I've run the race. I've faced more outlaws that most people can imagine, even given my reputation. I've faced them one at a time, and I've faced them in groups. I've faced men and women and aliens. I've put my life on the line more times than I can count. I've looked Death in the eye—and you know something? He's not a desperado holding a gun; he's me, Jefferson Nighthawk, with cheek-bones sticking out through his flesh and skin the texture of sandpaper. I've done more than society has any right to ask me, and now I want to enjoy what time is left to me. Is that so goddamned much to ask?"

"No, it's not," she said seriously. "But I know you, maybe better than you know yourself. And I know what will and won't make you happy."

"If you think killing makes me happy . . ." he began.

"No, I believe you when you say it doesn't," she replied. "But keep the job anyway. You probably won't have to do anything more than lock up an occasional drunk, or arrest someone for illegal parking." Suddenly she laughed. "Or maybe close the Sand Castle for watering its drinks. But at least you won't wither away from boredom."

"After the life I've lived, withering away from boredom looks mighty appealing."

"You won't think so once you give it a try."

"There's nothing boring about a book," he said. "Or about being with a good woman."

"I'm flattered that you think so, and I hope you'll still think so a year from now, but—"

"I'm not looking just one year ahead," said Nighthawk. "I intend to spend the rest of my life here—and I'm planning on living a lot longer than a year."

"If a thousand outlaws couldn't kill you and eplasia couldn't kill you, I personally can't see any reason why you shouldn't live forever."

"Forever would be nice. I'll settle for seventy-five. Until I get there. Then I'll shoot for ninety."

"Twenty-eight years of lying on hammocks and looking at birds," she said. "Is that really what you want?"

"Maybe we'll do a little traveling," he said. "I was always so busy looking into shadows that I never saw what was out there in the sunlight."

"Speaking of sunlight," said Sarah, looking out the window, "I see that it's getting light out." She paused. "We might as well get dressed. I'm too wide awake to go back to sleep."

"Me, too," said Nighthawk, getting to his feet and following her into the bedroom.

They emerged, fully clothed, a few minutes later, just in time to hear footsteps shuffling up the stone path to the house.

"Good morning," said Kinoshita as Nighthawk walked across the living room and opened the door. "I saw your light on, so I figured you were awake."

"You're not going to make a daily habit of showing up at sunrise, are you?" asked Nighthawk.

"No," answered Kinoshita. "I just came by to give you something you left behind."

Nighthawk stared at him curiously.

"I thought this might come in handy," said Kinoshita, pulling Nighthawk's discarded badge out of his pocket and handing it to him.

"You, too?" said Nighthawk irritably.

"Tumbleweed needs a lawman, and you're the best." Kinoshita grinned. "After last night, the city fathers won't consider anyone else."

"I don't *want* to be a lawman!"

"You can't always have what you want. I'd take the job, but I'm not half as good as you, and we both know it." Kinoshita paused. "Besides, it'll keep you from getting bored."

"Did you two plot this out while I was at the spaceport?" demanded Nighthawk.

"No, but if she's urging you to take back the badge, I approve," said Kinoshita.

"Why?"

"On practical grounds. Word of what happened last night at the spaceport is going to get out. The bad guys will know someone wiped out one of their crews, and the good guys are already bragging about the law-man they hired. Whether you stay or go, someone's go-ing to come after you. Maybe the drug runners' boss. Maybe his hired guns. Maybe some punk kids who want to test themselves against the lawman who killed four-teen bad guys at one time. But count on it: *someone's* going to come after you." He paused. "You might as well have the force of the law on your side."

Nighthawk looked slowly from Sarah to Kino-shita, then back again.

"You really think it's a good idea?" he asked her.

"I do."

He stared at the badge for a very long moment, then sighed deeply and bonded it to his tunic.

Chapter 17

• • • • • • • •

◈

It was almost two months before the first of them showed up.

Two idyllic months. It was the first time in his memory that Nighthawk was able to relax completely. He spent his days birding, reading, and working around the house. He built a deck off the kitchen, and a gazebo by the brook that ran behind the property. Then, because he was a realist, he also built a shooting range, where he practiced daily with his Burner, his Screecher, and his other weapons.

He also got his weight back up to where it had been more than a century ago, and none of it was fat. Sarah remarked that no one could eat as many calories as she was feeding him without turning soft as putty, but he worked them off almost as fast as he took them in.

True, he was the planet's official lawman, but it was such a peaceful little world that all he did was walk up and down the major streets once a day, check with the store owners to see if they had any complaints, and keep his office neat. About once a week he had to arrest a drunk, and a month into his tenure he broke up a fight, but that was the extent of it. He basically left Kinoshita to watch the office and call him if anything required his attention, and was grateful that almost nothing did.

"How long do you think it can last?" he said one day at breakfast.

"I thought you were happy here," answered Sarah, visibly upset. "Are you thinking of leaving?"

"I didn't ask how long *we* could last," he said reassuringly. "I was just wondering how long it'll be before they start showing up on Tumbleweed."

" *'They?'* "

"The gunmen, the kids out to make a reputation, the men who want to be able to brag that they killed the Widowmaker."

"We're pretty far off the beaten track," she replied. "Why should anyone come here?"

"Well, I did take out a sizable portion of the drug cartel's muscle," responded Nighthawk. "Most kingpins can't let something like that go unchallenged. And I have a feeling your city fathers are bragging about the new cop on the beat, rather than going out of their way to keep his identity a secret."

"I told them not to."

"So did I." He smiled. "That probably held them in check for all of five minutes."

"So that's why you practice on those targets every day."

"It's going to happen sooner or later. I might as well be prepared for it." He looked over at her. "I'm enjoying every minute I spend with you. I plan to die only with the greatest reluctance."

"Well," said Sarah, "if Jefferson Nighthawk doesn't want to die, I don't suppose there's anyone in the galaxy who can kill him."

"That may have been true when I was twenty-five or thirty."

"I'm tired of you constantly referring to your age!" she said irritably. "You've accomplished things since you came out of the hospital that are beyond almost any man half your age."

"Half my age is eighty-seven," he said with a smile.

"Maybe I ought to treat you like an old man," she said. "Maybe I should leave you completely alone on the assumption that any excitement might bring on a stroke or a heart attack."

"You never know," he answered. "It might."

"Oh, shut up."

"Of course, it might not. Maybe we ought to go into the next room and find out which, just out of curiosity."

"In a long lifetime of being propositioned," said Sarah, "I think that may very well be the least romantic invitation I ever had." Suddenly she smiled. "Let's go and find out."

Nighthawk got to his feet. "Sounds good to me."

And then his communicator chimed.

"Ito, you can pick the damnedest times to bother me," he said in annoyed tones as Kinoshita's holograph appeared in the air in front of him.

"We've got a pair of young toughs who plan to bother you a lot more than I can," said Kinoshita's.

"Any paper on them?"

"Not that I can find."

"And they've said they're after me?"

"Not in so many words—but you take one look at them and they're all adrenaline and testosterone and weapons . . . and why else could they be here?"

"Where are they now?"

"The Long Bar at the Sand Castle."

"Okay, they'll keep for an hour."

"You're not coming right away?"

"Soon. Let me know if they leave."

"Okay, you got it."

They broke the communication, and Nighthawk

turned back to Sarah, who had paused by the bedroom door, listening to him.

"Now, where were we?" he said.

"You're kidding!" she replied incredulously.

"Do I look like I'm kidding?"

"But there are two men in town who've come to kill you!"

"Then this might be my last time," he said with a grin. "I hope you'll make it memorable."

"I can't believe it! How can you think about sex at a time like this?"

"What better time to think about it?"

"Most men would be worried about a pair of killers who were up to no good."

"Most men haven't been in this situation a couple of hundred times. I have."

She stared at him, frowning. "Every time I think I understand you, something like this happens and I realize I don't know you at all."

He sighed in resignation. "You really want me to go to town right this minute?"

"Hell, no! For all I know, it *might* be our last time." She paused. "I just don't know how you can concentrate on it."

"Well, you know us old guys—we can't think of more than one thing at a time."

"You say that once more and I *will* send you to town."

So he didn't, and she didn't, and later he got dressed again as she watched him from the bed.

"If you don't come back, I want you to know that I love you."

"I'll be back," he said. "There are men out there who can kill me, but they're all old enough to shave."

"Aren't you even a little bit concerned?"

"I didn't get this far by not respecting what any man with a weapon can do," he said. "But I know what *I* can do, too."

He bound his laser holster to his trousers after checking the Burner's battery, then tucked a Screecher into his belt under his tunic, and slid a knife into each boot.

"I'll be back in a little while," he said, walking to the doorway.

"I'll be here."

He got into the vehicle and drove to his office, where Kinoshita was waiting for him.

"Are they still in the Sand Castle?" he asked.

"Yes."

"Good," he said, sitting down and putting his feet up on his desk. "Let's give them another half hour."

"They're not going away," said Kinoshita. "Why not get it over with now?"

"They're in the Long Bar," replied Nighthawk. "My guess is that they're not drinking milk. As long as they want to fuck up their reaction times, I see no reason to stop them."

Kinoshita grinned. "I never thought of that."

"Did you check with Customs at the spaceport and find out who the hell they are?"

"You're not going to believe their names."

"Try me."

"Are you ready for this? They call themselves Billy Danger and the Lightning Kid."

Nighthawk laughed aloud. "You're kidding."

"I couldn't make up anything that ludicrous on the spur of the moment."

"I suppose not," agreed Nighthawk. "They were probably Billy Smith and Freddie Jones six months ago, skipping classes and chasing girls." He paused. "Too bad they had to come here. They're just begging for *someone* to kill them, walking around with those names." He shook his head. "Billy Danger."

"Watch out for the other one."

"The Lightning Kid?" asked Nighthawk. He chuckled. "My God, it's hard to say that name with a straight face."

"I think he's on something."

"Oh?"

"Twitches a lot. Wall-to-wall pupils. Billy Danger looks nervous as all hell, like he got talked into this. But the other one, there's something about him: he looks like torturing small animals is his favorite hobby."

"Okay, when they come out of there, let me know which is which."

"You'll know," said Kinoshita with absolute conviction.

And sure enough, when the two young men emerged from the Sand Castle twenty minutes later, Nighthawk had no trouble spotting the Lightning Kid. He seemed almost brighter than the sun, dressed in metallic gold: tunic, pants, even belt, boots, and holsters. He wore a silver scarf around his neck, and skintight silver gloves. Nighthawk fought back the urge to laugh for a few seconds, then gave in to it.

"What do you think?" said Kinoshita.

"He looks like a fashion designer's worst nightmare."

"And the other one?"

Nighthawk looked at Billy Danger. He was flamboyantly dressed, though not compared to his companion. His shirt had oversized, puffy sleeves, his polished, shining boots came up almost to his knees, and his weapons would cost an average man a year's pay.

"Typical," said Nighthawk. "No surprises here."

"You sound like you've seen them before."

"A thousand times."

"You want me to stand with you?"

Nighthawk shook his head. "No paper on 'em, remember? You kill them, I have to arrest you."

"Just deputize me."

"Someday I will. But not for a couple of kids just out of diapers."

Nighthawk walked out the door and stood in the street, waiting for the two young men to approach him.

"Good morning," he said when they were about

forty feet away. "I'm told that you have some business with me?"

"You can't be *him*!" said the Lightning Kid, obviously disappointed. "Look at you! You're an old man, and you're dressed just like everyone else."

"I know this is going to come as a shock to you," said Nighthawk, "but they don't give out a prize for the flashiest-dressed killer on the Frontier."

"It's him," said Billy Danger nervously. "I've seen holos of him. He's older, but it's him."

"You're sure?" asked the Lightning Kid, swaying slightly and trying to focus his eyes on Nighthawk.

"Believe me, it's the Widowmaker!" answered Billy Danger, and Nighthawk noticed a slight trembling in his hands.

"And now that you've seen me, why don't you go back home while you still can?"

"We're going to be the men who killed the Widowmaker," said the Lightning Kid.

"Go home now, and someday you may even grow up to become men."

"I want to see if you're as good as they say."

"Better," answered Nighthawk. He concentrated on Billy Danger. "Don't do anything foolish, kid. Have you ever killed anyone before?"

"Sure," blustered Billy Danger. "Lots of men."

"Bullshit. You're shaking like a leaf. I want you to consider something, kid: This is old hat to me. I've been facing young guns for more than a century, and I'm still here. I *know* what I can do. Until you know you can beat the Widowmaker, maybe you'd better go home and think seriously about what you mean to do."

Billy Danger was silent for a moment, as if he was actually considering Nighthawk's suggestion. Finally he spoke. "I can't. People will laugh."

"They won't laugh at your funeral. Is that what you want?"

"I've got to think about it."

"Don't take too long," said Nighthawk, walking a few steps closer.

"Hold it right there!" bellowed the Lightning Kid.

"Okay," said Nighthawk, stopping. "What now?"

"You're not going to talk *me* out of this!"

"I'm not even going to try," said Nighthawk. "It'll be a pleasure to kill you."

The young man frowned and blinked his eyes. "You can't kill me. I'm the Lightning Kid!"

"If *I* can't kill you, then the man in my office who's got his laser rifle trained on you certainly will."

"Where?" asked the Lightning Kid, turning awkwardly and trying to pinpoint Nighthawk's office window. As he did so, Nighthawk whipped out his Burner and melted both of the Kid's weapons in their holsters, then turned his gun on the other young man.

"Billy Danger, you've got to the count of five to pull your weapon or leave. It's your choice."

"Holster your weapon," said Billy Danger.

"My planet, my rules. The Burner stays out. One, two . . ."

"All right, all right—I'm leaving," said Billy Danger.

"And leave your weapons on the ground."

"But they cost my . . . *me*—"

"Consider it an object lesson."

Billy Danger seemed to be reconsidering, but before his hand could snake down toward his weapon, he took another look at the Burner that was trained on him and quickly unbound his holsters. They slid to the ground, and he began walking away.

"Spaceport's the other direction," said Nighthawk.

The young man turned and began walking again.

"I know it's painful, and a little humiliating," said Nighthawk. "You might remember that the next time you consider killing someone who never did you any harm."

Billy Danger didn't answer, but simply increased

his pace, and Nighthawk turned his attention back to the Lightning Kid.

"What about you?" he said. "Are you willing to walk back to the spaceport?"

"Sure," said the Kid with a crazed laugh. "But I'll be back."

"I don't think so," said Nighthawk.

"You think melting a couple of guns will stop the Lightning Kid?"

"Probably not," admitted Nighthawk.

"Damned right, Widowmaker. Hell, I can always get more guns."

"Yeah, I suppose you can—but you'll need to learn how to fire them without a trigger finger." He burned away the Kid's two forefingers, as the young man screamed in pain. "I know it hurts—but remember, I could have killed you. After all, you came here to kill *me*."

"I'll get you for this!" yelled the Lightning Kid.

"Sure you will," said Nighthawk, unimpressed. "Now get the hell out of here before I get really mad at you."

The Lightning Kid, trying to clutch the stumps of his blackened, smoking forefingers, staggered past Nighthawk. As he did so, Nighthawk saw a movement out of the corner of his eye, and ducked just as Billy Danger, tears of fright and humiliation mingling on his cheeks, dove for him with a gleaming knife in his hand.

The blade opened a wound on Nighthawk's shoulder, and the shock made him drop his Burner.

"I'm sorry!" babbled Billy Danger. "I don't want to do this! But he's my partner—I've got to stand up for him!"

"He's an asshole," said Nighthawk, turning to face him. "You don't owe him a thing. You can still walk away."

"I wish I could, but I can't!"

Billy Danger charged again, and Nighthawk side-stepped and delivered a killing blow to the back of his neck. The young man fell to the street without a sound.

At exactly that instant, the Lightning Kid dove for the Burner Nighthawk had dropped. Nighthawk kicked him full in the face, and as the Kid sprawled on the ground the gun went flying. Nighthawk pulled his Screecher out of his belt and pointed it at the Kid.

"A very misguided boy is dead because of you," he grated. "I wouldn't mind blowing you away as well, so get up very slowly and don't make any sudden moves." The Kid looked at the Burner, which lay on the ground a few feet away. "Don't even think about it," continued Nighthawk. "Even if you reached it before I shot you, how are you going to fire the damned thing?"

And then, suddenly, with no warning, the Lightning Kid went berserk. He uttered an animal scream of rage and hurled himself at Nighthawk, who brought him up short with a stiff blow to the breastbone. The Kid shrieked, but never backed away, and began clawing manically at Nighthawk's face. The older man tried to sidestep, but found that he wasn't as quick as he'd thought he was, and an instant later the Kid's fingernails were raking the skin off his face. Nighthawk ducked, delivered two blows that would have stopped anyone who wasn't out of his mind on drugs and adrenaline, and the Kid dropped to his knees. But he was up a second later, this time with Billy Danger's wicked-looking knife in his hand, and he brought it down with all his strength, aiming at Nighthawk's chest.

What happened next was sheer instinct. Nighthawk's hand shot out, and the heel of it caught the Kid's nose, driving the bone and cartilage into the brain. The Kid screamed one last time, the knife dropped from his bloody hand, and he collapsed at Nighthawk's feet.

Kinoshita raced up to Nighthawk a moment later. "Nice job," he said.

"It was a fucking clumsy job," said Nighthawk disgustedly. "I shouldn't have had to kill the first one. I didn't even mean to kill *this* one, but I wasn't quick enough to take him out *without* killing him."

"It's over, and you're alive," said Kinoshita. "That's all that matters."

"It's just beginning," muttered Nighthawk. He looked at the two corpses and grimaced. "Shit!" he said unhappily. "This isn't the way it was supposed to be."

Chapter 18

❖ ❖ ❖ ❖ ❖ ❖ ❖ ❖

He was a hero to all the planetary officials, who didn't hesitate to spread the word that Tumbleweed was now under the protection of the notorious Widowmaker. He tried to explain to them that this was hardly the way to keep reputation-seeking young guns away from the planet, but in their eyes he was everything legend had made him out to be: after all, he'd killed fourteen men single-handedly at the spaceport, and in case anyone doubted his abilities, he killed a pair of young toughs right out on Main Street in front of everyone.

Let them come with their best, was the officials' attitude; *we've* got the Widowmaker.

"They're fools," he muttered, for perhaps the thousandth time, while he was having breakfast with Sarah.

"Probably," she agreed. "But it's too late to do anything about it."

"We can leave."

"Tumbleweed is my home," she responded. "I don't want to leave."

"Neither do I. But they don't realize what's going to happen. I'm not sure even you do."

"A few guns will show up."

He shook his head. "Every ambitious killer on the Frontier will show up," he corrected her. "It used to happen every time I stayed in one place too long more than a century ago, and thanks to a bunch of hack writers and phony documentaries I'm more famous today that I was back then."

"It's been three weeks since you killed Billy Danger and the Lightning Kid," she said. "No one's showed up."

"It takes time for word to get around. They'll show up, all right. And they won't all be kids. Some of them will be men I can't take."

"You can take anyone."

"You, too?" he said irritably. "Trust me, I know my limitations."

"You're being too modest," she said. "But I'll make this concession: The day you feel someone has come to Tumbleweed to kill you, someone you think might succeed, I'll leave with you. Fair enough?"

"Fair enough."

"You know, you do have an advantage here that you never had before."

"You?"

"Me?" She chuckled and shook her head. "I was referring to Kinoshita. No one knows him, which means no one knows he's working for you."

"He puzzles me," said Nighthawk.

"Why?"

"Because I don't know who the hell he's working for, but it's not me. He was there at the hospital when I woke up, and he's been at my side ever since, but I'll be damned if I know why, and it bothers me."

"Maybe he just likes you."

Nighthawk smiled wryly. "I'm not that likable."

"I think you are."

He shook his head. "I give him orders. I don't listen to his advice. I get him into the damnedest scrapes. There's no reason why he should stick around."

"Why don't you ask him?"

"I have."

"And he hasn't answered?"

"Not exactly. He admits he's got a reason for being with me, but he hasn't told me what it is." Nighthawk paused. "When the time comes, I'll demand it."

"When will that be?"

He shrugged. "I can't tell you. But I'll know it when it's here."

They finished breakfast, then drove out to the countryside, where they took their daily walk through the woods. They spent a few hours looking at birds and identifying flowers—another new hobby—and then went back to town. After dropping her at the restaurant, Nighthawk parked the vehicle and began making his rounds.

All went routinely until he stopped at one of the smaller hotels.

"Good morning," he greeted the desk clerk.

"Good morning, Jefferson," came the reply. "Did those men find you?"

"What men?"

"Three men. They checked in, then asked where they could find you."

"Did they ask for Jefferson Nighthawk, or for the Widowmaker?"

"I can't really remember," admitted the clerk. "Is it important?"

"Probably not. Thanks."

Nighthawk walked back to his office, where he found Kinoshita doing some paperwork.

"Hi. What's up?"

"Three men are looking for me. Do you know who they are, or why they want to find me?"

"I can't know every enemy the two clones made,"

answered Kinoshita. "The first one went off on his own
the second he hit the Frontier, and the second one got a
few million people mad at him."

"Well, just the same, I want you to wander around
town until you run into them and then tell me if you
recognize them," said Nighthawk.

"What difference does it make?" asked Kinoshita.
"If they're looking for you, there's just one reason."

"Because before I kill a man, or get killed by him,
I'd like to know why."

"You know why—right now you're the biggest
trophy on the Frontier."

"Maybe I can convince them that the bad guys are
supposed to be the trophies."

"If they're here to kill you, they *are* the bad guys,"
answered Kinoshita.

"Just do what I say."

"You're the boss," said Kinoshita, getting up and
walking to the door. "Have you got any idea where
they're supposed to be right now?"

"Looking for me."

"They can't be too bright, or they'd have come
right to the office." Kinoshita walked out the door and
down the street while Nighthawk sat at his desk.

He had his computer pull the guest registrations
from the hotel, after which he scanned their faces
and names. There were five or six possibilities, but he
couldn't recognize any of them, and he didn't have the
budget or the patience to tie into the Master Computer
on Deluros VIII and try to learn more about them.

Kinoshita returned about half an hour later.

"Well?"

"I found them. They're eating at your ladyfriend's
place."

"Do they know she's my ladyfriend, as you so
delicately put it?"

"I don't think so," answered Kinoshita. "I think
they're just hungry."

"Do you know them?"

Kinoshita shook his head. "I never saw any of them before—which doesn't mean that they aren't from Tundra or Pericles. I mean, after all, there's no paper on you, and I can't imagine anyone's put out a hit on you."

"Paper's got nothing to do with it," answered Nighthawk. "If you want to get famous fast, you kill the Widowmaker."

"Well, what do you want to do about them?"

"They're not breaking any laws. Let's leave them alone for a while."

"These aren't like those kids you killed last month," said Kinoshita. "They're not going to get so drunk they're useless in a fight."

"Can you tell me anything about them?" asked Nighthawk. "Anything at all?"

"Just that they're tough-looking men, Jefferson. You may make their reputations, but I've got a feeling you're not the first man they've gone up against."

Nighthawk stood up. "Okay, then, I suppose I'd better go do something about them."

"I'll come with you."

"As you wish."

"You never let me join you before," noted Kinoshita.

"I always knew who my enemies were before. I don't want to confront the wrong men."

"Oh," said Kinoshita, visibly disappointed.

"You're a good man," said Nighthawk. "I don't want you getting killed on my account. I just want you to identify them."

"It would be an honor to die with the Widowmaker."

"First, I'm not the Widowmaker, and second, dying is never an honor. The object of the exercise is to kill the other guy."

They began walking toward the restaurant. Then, when they were half a block away, Nighthawk came to a dead stop.

"What is it?" asked Kinoshita.

"I just had a thought," he said.

"Oh?"

"Yeah. Let's go through the kitchen."

"Whatever you say."

They walked around to the back of the restaurant and entered through the service door.

"Hi," said Sarah, walking over to him. "I didn't expect to see you again till dinner."

Nighthawk signaled for silence, then walked to the doorway to the restaurant. There were three lean, dark-clad men sitting at a table by the front door.

"Are those the men?" he whispered.

Kinoshita nodded.

"Wait here," he said, and walked out the service door. He was back in less than a minute.

"What are they drinking?"

"Coffee," answered Sarah.

"Bring me a fresh pot."

She did as he asked. He lifted the top and dropped five small pills into it.

"What was that?" she asked.

"That was a gunfight-avoider I borrowed from the pharmacy," said Nighthawk. "There's enough in those pills to put a platoon to sleep, let alone three men. Take it out and leave it on the table. Don't offer to pour. I don't want them thinking anyone's anxious for them to drink."

Sarah took the container, walked out into the restaurant and over to the three men before anyone could ask for a refill, and left the pot in the middle of their table.

"Now what?" whispered Kinoshita.

"Now you go to the doctor's office. Get three airsleds and bring them back here. We'll need them to cart these guys off to jail."

"They haven't broken any laws, you know."

"Then I probably can't hold them more than a year or two, can I?" replied Nighthawk.

Kinoshita shrugged, walked out the back, and began hunting up the airsleds. Nighthawk poured himself a cup of coffee, sat down on a stool, and sipped it, as Sarah kept watch on the three men. For the longest time it seemed to her that they were never going to refill their cups, but finally they did, and within a minute all three seemed to be talking and gesticulating in slow motion.

She reported their behavior to Nighthawk, who walked into the restaurant just as they were losing consciousness, assured the other patrons that there was nothing to worry about, and laid the three men gently on the floor.

Kinoshita showed up a few minutes later with the airsleds. He and Nighthawk lifted each man onto a sled, then ushered them out the front door and over to the jail, where Nighthawk disarmed them and locked all three of them in a single cell.

"How long are they out for?" asked Kinoshita, staring at the three motionless men.

"Maybe three hours, maybe four. I'll be back in late afternoon to have a little chat with them. Give them water if they ask for it; nothing else."

"No food?"

"I wouldn't want them to be too comfortable when I speak to them," said Nighthawk.

"Where will you be if I need you?"

"You won't."

"But *if* I do."

"I'll be taking a nap at Sarah's place."

"You can sleep at a time like this?" asked Kinoshita incredulously.

"I've just had a strenuous morning of bird-watching and not killing three men," said Nighthawk with just the trace of a smile. "That's about all a man of my advanced years can handle before lunch."

Chapter 19

◆　◆　◆　◆　◆　◆　◆　◆

"*Good afternoon,*" *said Nighthawk, sitting comfortably on* a chair just outside the cell. "How are we feeling?"

"Like shit warmed over," groaned one of the three men, holding his head. "What the hell was in that coffee?"

"A little something that any doctor could lose his license for prescribing," answered Nighthawk with a smile.

"Why are we here?" asked another of the men.

"I thought we should have a little chat."

"What about?"

"Life. Death. Things like that."

"If you're going to kill us, get it over with," said the man. "But don't talk us to death."

"If I wanted to kill you," said Nighthawk, "I could have done it this morning."

"Why didn't you?"

"It would just attract more scum to Tumbleweed. We want to be left alone here." He paused. "More to the point, *I* want to be left alone." He stared at the three men. "You came here to kill me. Was it your own idea, or did someone hire you?"

The three men looked at each other. Finally the first of them shrugged and turned back to Nighthawk.

"It was our idea."

"Why?"

Silence.

Nighthawk pointed a pistol at them. "You're in a lousy bargaining position. I want an answer."

"All right," said the nearest man. "We're for hire, and the men who killed the Widowmaker can charge top prices."

"Do you know why?"

The man stared at him, but offered no reply.

"You'd command a higher price because men have been trying to kill me for a century and a half, and I'm still here." Nighthawk's contempt for their abilities was reflected in his expression. "Did you ever stop to ask yourself why that should be, why so many men have tried to kill me and none have succeeded?"

"We know you're good. That's why there are three of us."

"Maybe you'd better take up a different profession," suggested Nighthawk. "You're not the brightest gunfighters I ever met. In fact, the only reason you're still alive is because you were dumb enough to come to my world and eat and drink everything that was put in front of you without testing it—not exactly a survival trait out here."

"The only reason *you're* alive is because you drugged us instead of facing us," said the largest of the men, speaking for the first time.

Nighthawk tossed a small, octagonal coin from the Hesperite system to the man. "Throw it at the wall over there."

The man caught the coin, stared curiously at Nighthawk for a moment, then shrugged and hurled the coin at the far wall of the cell. Nighthawk, without ever getting out of his chair, drew his Burner and melted the coin in midair.

"I'm just as good with my other hand," he said. "Maybe even better. Now, do you *really* want to face me?"

There were no answers, but they were unable to hide their sudden reluctance.

"I'll interpret that as a negative answer," continued Nighthawk. "Now, if I let you out of your cell and point you toward the spaceport, can I reasonably expect you to get the hell off the planet and never return?"

More silence. Finally the largest man nodded his head.

"What about our weapons?"

"They're on your ship. The power packs stay here."

"Power packs cost money."

"So do triple funerals," replied Nighthawk. "Do you want to pay for new packs, or have Tumbleweed pay for the funerals?"

The men glared at him, but offered no response.

Nighthawk uttered the code that opened the cell.

The three men walked to the door. Two of them walked out in the street. The third, who hadn't spoken at all, turned to Nighthawk, his body tense.

"Don't even think of it," said Nighthawk.

"You're an old man. Get rid of those weapons and I can take you."

"I doubt it—but I didn't get to be an old man by accepting stupid challenges."

"The Widowmaker's backing down?" said the man contemptuously.

"The Widowmaker's offering you your life," replied Nighthawk. "A smart man would take it and leave."

The man didn't move. "I could have taken you with a gun, too."

"Sure you could."

"Anyone can melt a coin with a Burner. You just spray the whole area."

"If you say so. Now get the hell out of here before I lock you up again."

"I'll be back, you know."

"That's fine by me. The cemetery won't be full for years yet."

The man glared at him for a long moment, then finally turned and walked out after his companions.

Nighthawk stood by his window, watching them until they caught the shuttle to the spaceport.

The man probably *would* be back. Nighthawk wondered if he'd have let him walk away a century ago, and concluded, to his surprise, that he probably wouldn't have.

The Widowmaker didn't believe in letting enemies live. He killed calmly and efficiently, without emotion, without regret. If a man came to a world to kill him, that man was, by definition, a mortal enemy, and the Widowmaker didn't allow mortal enemies to live.

The Widowmaker also didn't second-guess himself—which he viewed as further proof that he was no longer the Widowmaker.

Chapter 20

Finally the men that Nighthawk had been expecting, ge-nerically at least, arrived on Tumbleweed.

He was sitting on Sarah's porch, reading a book, when she came out from town to speak to him.

"What's the problem?" he asked. "You look troubled."

"It's time to leave."

"You're throwing me out?"

"I'm coming with you," she replied. "We're both leaving this world."

"What the hell's going on?"

"We always knew the time would come," said Sarah. "Well, it's here. Let's pack up and go."

Nighthawk put the book down on a small table and got to his feet. "I'll go when I'm ready," he said. "And I don't feel ready yet. I want to know what put this scare into you."

"All right," she said, looking into his eyes. "Two men came to Tumbleweed. They haven't said that they're here for you, but that has to be the reason."

"Men have come here for me before."

"Not like these two," she said.

"Tell me about them."

"There's nothing to tell," answered Sarah. "There's just something about them. You take one look and you know they're born killers."

"They're probably a couple of businessmen who dressed up to impress the locals," said Nighthawk.

"Don't humor me, Jefferson," said Sarah. "I've seen them come and go, and I've never seen anyone like these two. Maybe you could have taken one of them in your prime, but . . ."

"This isn't like you," said Nighthawk. "Usually you're the one who wants me to go slay dragons for you, and I'm the reluctant knight."

"These dragons are different."

"You don't mind if I go see for myself?"

"The hell I don't!" she snapped. "If you go into town, you'll never come back!"

"I appreciate your confidence," he replied ironically.

"I spent a long time waiting for someone like you," she said. "I don't want to lose you this soon."

"I've got to at least see them, you know."

"I'm begging you not to."

"Tell you what," he said, removing his holster and laying his various pistols down next to the book. "I'll leave all my weapons here. They won't enhance their reputations by shooting down an unarmed man."

"I have a feeling their reputations don't *need* enhancing," she replied.

He walked over to the vehicle. "I'll be back soon."

"I hope so."

"But you doubt it?"

"You're the best I've ever seen . . . but they're what you were thirty years ago."

"Thirty years ago I was a skeleton in a cryonics chamber," he responded. "I didn't go through all that so I could be shot down on the streets of Tumbleweed."

He got into the vehicle and took off for town. He decided not to park at his office—there was no sense announcing his identity to whoever might be looking for him—so he parked well past the Sand Castle and began walking slowly down the street. He looked into the restaurant to see if the men who had so frightened Sarah were there, but there was just a pair of elderly women having tea.

Finally he walked to Tavern Row, a stretch of the street that held three taverns in a row, and looked into the first. Things seemed pretty dull—a few drinkers, a couple of men and a Canphorite playing *jabob*. The second tavern hadn't even opened for business yet.

He walked into the third, which was relatively crowded for this early in the day, and saw two elegantly tailored gray-clad men standing at the bar, each wearing tight-fitting custom-made gloves. Even though they were motionless, there was a certain grace about them, a potential that was immediately evident.

Nighthawk walked to a table, sat down, ordered a beer off the holographic menu, and studied the two men.

"Your name Nighthawk?" asked one of the men, staring at him in the mirror behind the bar.

"That's right."

"Then I insist that you let us pick up the tab for that beer."

"Whatever makes you happy," answered Nighthawk.

"I think it'd make us happy to join you at your table."

"Be my guest."

"Thanks. We will."

The two men walked over and sat down on each side of him.

"I'm Mr. Dark," said the one who had been speaking. "This is my friend, Mr. Night."

"Night and Nighthawk," offered Mr. Night. "Maybe we're related."

"Anything's possible."

"No, there are certain things that aren't possible," said Mr. Night. "Would you like an example?"

"If you insist."

"It's not possible that you can survive a fight with us."

"If you say so."

"You're allowed to disagree," said Mr. Dark, dabbing at this mouth with a silk handkerchief. "In fact, you could come out into the street and disagree with us right now, if you're so inclined."

Nighthawk held his arms out from his body. "I certainly can't survive a fight while I'm unarmed."

"I've heard stories that you're just as good without a weapon."

"I might have been once, but that was a long time ago. You wouldn't get much pleasure giving a beating to a feeble old man like me."

"No one else in this town seems to think you're all that feeble."

"That's because they hope you'll come after me instead of them," said Nighthawk with a smile.

"And that's just what we've done."

"I can't imagine why."

"Surely you're kidding!" said Mr. Dark.

"Not at all," said Nighthawk. "If you win, they'll say you can kill a tired old man, and if you lose, they'll say you can't. Either way, what good will it do you?"

"I have a feeling that Mr. Nighthawk doesn't take us seriously, Mr. Dark," said Mr. Night.

"Perhaps he needs a demonstration, Mr. Night," suggested Mr. Dark.

Before Nighthawk could respond, they had each whipped out their Burners and melted off the tops of some fifty bottles of bar stock without their beams of deadly light hitting anything else or doing any damage to the rest of the place. The entire demonstration took less than two seconds from start to finish.

"What do you think, Mr. Nighthawk?" asked Mr. Dark as customers who had thrown themselves to the floor began getting up and looking around, trying to figure out exactly what had happened.

"I think we'll probably have to add all that to your bar bill."

"He's still not taking us seriously, Mr. Night," said Mr. Dark.

"I suppose the only way to get his attention is to break some laws, Mr. Dark," replied his companion.

"Or possibly kill a friend or two of his," agreed Mr. Dark. He turned to Nighthawk. "I wonder: Does a man like you have any friends?"

"Not many," admitted Nighthawk. "But you know that. It goes with the territory."

"True," answered Mr. Dark.

"Just out of curiosity, who sent you?" asked Nighthawk.

"No one," said Mr. Night.

"Then why are you here?" continued Nighthawk. "What did I ever do to you?"

"You got here first."

Nighthawk nodded thoughtfully. "Good answer."

"I'm glad you approve," said Mr. Night. "Perhaps you'll show your appreciation by taking us up on our offer."

"Not right now."

"Sooner or later you'll have to, you know," said Mr. Dark.

"Later, I think."

"If you're frightened, you might consider calling just one of us out," said Mr. Night. "Either one of us. It makes no difference."

"Will the other want to give up all credit for killing the Widowmaker?" asked Nighthawk.

"We're a team, Mr. Nighthawk," said Mr. Dark. "We share in all things."

"That must startle your ladyfriends from time to time," suggested Nighthawk.

"We don't have any ladyfriends."

"Oh?"

"Like I said, we're a team. Each of us is all the other needs."

Mr. Night stared at Nighthawk. "I think he disapproves of us, Mr. Dark."

"Probably, Mr. Night," agreed Mr. Dark. He turned to Nighthawk. "The cemeteries are filled with men who disapproved of us."

"I don't doubt it," said Nighthawk. His hand, which had been resting on his knee, slipped gently down to the top of his boot, where his knife was concealed. He considered pulling it out, but knew he wasn't fast enough to kill them both, or probably even one, before they shot him, not even with the element of surprise in his favor. When he was twenty, or thirty, he'd have tried; at forty, probably . . . but not now.

They didn't frighten him the way they terrified Sarah. He'd been dealing with men like this all his life. He wasn't afraid to face them, and he wasn't afraid to die—but he couldn't see any reason to throw his life away, and he knew that's what he'd be doing if he took them on. He would never admit it to them, but their demonstration of their skills had been *that* impressive. In his youth he might have been the tiniest fraction of a second faster, the slightest degree more accurate . . . but his youth was farther in the past than most men's, and he was realist enough to know that he couldn't take Mr. Dark or Mr. Night today, not even if he were armed and facing them on his own terms.

"I suppose we could try to humiliate him in front of all the people here who seem to worship him," said Mr. Dark.

"I don't know," replied Mr. Night. "Mr. Nighthawk

strikes me as a man who has no quality of shame. I don't think he *can* be humiliated."

"Perhaps you're right," agreed Mr. Dark. "Of course, we'll never know until we try."

"He *is* the only lawman on Tumbleweed," noted Mr. Night. "Maybe we should break some laws and see what happens."

"He'd probably have to arrest us," said Mr. Dark.

"Really?" said Mr. Night, pulling out his Screecher and aiming it at the huge mirror behind the bar. He pulled the trigger and the mirror shattered into a thousand pieces. "You mean he might want to arrest me for something as innocent and fun-loving as that?"

"You never can tell," said Mr. Dark as pandemonium ensued and the bartender and all the customers fled into the street.

"He hasn't arrested me yet," said Mr. Night. "Maybe if I shot some innocent bystanders . . ."

"Oh, I don't think that will be necessary, will it, Mr. Nighthawk?" said Mr. Dark. "I think you'll go home, confront your demons, and face us later today, won't you?"

"I'd say it's a pretty strong possibility," said Nighthawk.

"I think it would be a good idea," continued Mr. Dark. "Because as you may well have guessed, we do have ways of getting the locals to tell us where you live. If we have to go to the trouble of seeking you out at your home, we'll probably be in such a foul mood that we'll burn it down and kill anyone who runs out of it."

"We mean anyone besides yourself, of course," added Mr. Night.

"Just out of curiosity, did you two burn down a house I had back on Churchill II?" asked Nighthawk.

"Someone has appropriated our methods?" said Mr. Dark, feigning shock. "I'm appalled."

"Of course it wasn't us," said Mr. Night. "The proof of it is that you're still alive."

Nighthawk got to his feet. "I assume you're not going anywhere?"

"Not until we do what we came here to do," answered Mr. Dark.

"I'll see you later, then."

"May I ask a question?"

"Be my guest."

"Why did you come here unarmed?"

"I like to scout out the opposition," said Nighthawk.

"And?"

"And now that I know I can beat you," he lied, "I'm going home to get my weapons."

For just a moment Mr. Dark looked unsure of himself. "Maybe we should kill you now."

"Maybe," agreed Nighthawk. "But you won't. How would it sound—two amateurs shoot down the king when he's not armed?"

"Leave," said Mr. Night. "We'll be waiting for you."

Nighthawk walked to the door, then out into the street and toward his vehicle. When he reached it, he entered it and drove it to Sarah's house, where Sarah and Kinoshita were waiting for him.

"I half-expected never to see you again," she said.

"I told you I'd be back."

"I contacted Ito and asked him to come out here. I hope that if I can't talk you into leaving, maybe he can."

"I've checked them out," said Kinoshita. "They hire out as a team. They've killed thirty-eight men between them."

"I can believe that," said Nighthawk. "They're pretty good. Almost as good as I used to be." He smiled wryly. "They gave me a demonstration."

"Can you take them?"

"Not a chance."

"Can *we* take them?" persisted Kinoshita.

Nighthawk shook his head. "Don't come back with me. You'd just be a cannon fodder."

"Well, if you know you can't beat them, let's get the hell off the planet," said Sarah.

Nighthawk looked at her for a long moment. "I'm tired of running. It's not my nature."

"But you admit they'll kill you."

"If I run, they'll just shoot up Tumbleweed. A lot of innocent people will die."

"The hell they will," said Sarah. "They want *you*, not Tumbleweed."

"Look," he said. "I'm not anxious to die. I've avoided fights before for what I thought were good reasons, and I wish I could avoid this one—but if I run, they'll follow me to the next world. And if they don't, then just about the time we build a house and decide to stay, someone just as deadly will show up. I want to live in peace, but I've already deserted Churchill and Pondoro; I'm not going to keep running the rest of my life. I had hoped I could live another twenty or thirty years, but if I can't, I can't. I've lived with Death for a long time; I'm not afraid of it. And who knows? Maybe they're not as good as they think, and maybe I'm better than you think."

He stared defiantly at Sarah. From somewhere behind him he heard Kinoshita's voice mutter "Jefferson, I'm sorry!" but before he could turn around, a gun barrel came down hard on his head, and he fell, unconscious, to the floor.

Chapter 21

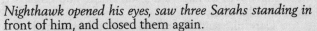

Nighthawk opened his eyes, saw three Sarahs standing in front of him, and closed them again.

"He's awake," he heard her say.

"Good," said Kinoshita. "For a minute there, I was afraid I'd done him some real harm."

Nighthawk reopened his left eye and was able to focus it just enough to see that he was inside his spaceship.

"What the hell happened?" he mumbled, trying to get to his feet, only to find that he was bound to a chair.

"I saved your life," said Kinoshita. "Of course, you may not view it that way, so I thought it might be best to restrain you until I could explain."

"What did you hit me with?" asked Nighthawk. "It felt like a piano."

"The barrel of a laser rifle," said Kinoshita. "Good

thing you're a rich man. That was a damned valuable weapon that will never work again."

"Here," said Sarah, placing a small pill in his mouth and holding a cup of water to his lips. "Swallow."

Nighthawk did as she said, and found, to his amazement, that his pain subsided and his vision cleared within half a minute.

"Better?" she asked.

He nodded, half expecting the motion to set off new agonies within his skull, but there was no discomfort.

"Okay," said Kinoshita, uttering a code that released the bonds. "You're free now."

"Why did you do it?" asked Nighthawk, tenderly touching the lump on the back of his head.

"You were about to commit suicide, remember?"

"I might have won."

"We both know you wouldn't have."

"It makes no difference," snapped Nighthawk. "You had no right—" He stood up, was overcome by alternating waves of nausea and dizziness, and collapsed back onto his chair.

"Careful," said Kinoshita. "That was a hell of a concussion. It'd be a good idea not to make any sudden movements for the next couple of days."

Nighthawk was silent for a moment, until the dizziness passed.

"Where are we heading?" he asked.

"I don't know," answered Kinoshita. "As soon as I make sure that your two friends aren't on our tail, we can discuss a location."

"You just tell us where to drop you," said Nighthawk. "We'll take it from there."

"No chance," said Kinoshita firmly. "We're partners, remember?"

"The hell we are. Partners don't whack partners with rifle barrels."

"That's some fucking gratitude after I stop you from getting your damned head blown off," said Kinoshita.

"Gratitude be damned," said Nighthawk. "You've been skirting the subject ever since I got out of the hospital, and now I want a straight answer or we part ways. Why have you attached yourself to me?"

Kinoshita stared at him for a long moment, trying to make up his mind.

"All right," he said at last. "I made a promise."

"To who?"

"To the Widowmaker."

"What are you talking about?" demanded Nighthawk. "*I'm* the Widowmaker."

"You weren't when I made it."

"Explain."

"It was on Pericles, just after your second clone killed Cassius Hill," said Kinoshita. "He gave me the money that would keep you alive."

"I know that."

"There was more, though. He knew you'd be an old man, and possibly a sick one—certainly one who was a century out of date. He asked me to watch over you, and I promised him that I would."

"Bullshit."

"I swear it's the truth."

"He had to know that even at sixty-two I could take you without drawing a deep breath. There's no way he would have asked you to protect me."

"I didn't say *protect*," shot back Kinoshita. "I trained the first clone, and I fought for the second. I've done whatever *you've* asked me to do. I *serve* the Widowmaker; this little incident on Tumbleweed is one of the very few times any of you have needed protection." He paused. "Now that the clone has changed his face and his name, and you're back on the Frontier, you're the Widowmaker again, and you're the man to whom I owe my allegiance."

"Are you in touch with this clone?"

"Not directly. I leave messages at a blind electronic address. I assume he picks them up."

Nighthawk sat in silence, considering what he'd

heard. Finally he looked at Kinoshita and spoke: "You serve the Widowmaker?"

"That's right."

"And that's me?"

"Yes."

"Then I want you to contact my clone and tell him that if he's not willing to be the Widowmaker anymore, you're through leaving messages for him."

"But—"

"If he's not the Widowmaker and I am, then your loyalty is to me, right?"

"Yes, but—"

"Then tell him you're all through sending messages. Wherever we wind up, I don't want *anyone* to know, not even him."

"You insist?"

"I do." He turned to Sarah. "Did you know about this?"

"No," she replied. "I'm as surprised as you are."

He looked at Kinoshita. "Okay, make up your mind: Are you serving *me* or *him*?"

"Despite your frequent protestations to the contrary, you're the Widowmaker again. I'm *your* man."

"Tell him I ordered you to cut off communications. No sense having him blame you for it."

Kinoshita nodded in assent.

"Maybe he'll seek you out himself, now that he can't keep tabs on you through Ito," suggested Sarah.

"He won't."

"How do you know?"

"It's difficult to explain," said Nighthawk. "Without me, there'd be no him. The reverse isn't true. I don't mind the thought of meeting him; he's very much like a son, from my viewpoint. But from his, I'm almost a god; he was created in my image, with my memories, for the sole purpose of keeping me alive. That was his mission, his only reason for existence." He sighed and shook his head. "No, he won't want to meet me in person." He glanced at Kinoshita. "Will he?"

"No, he absolutely refuses." Suddenly he smiled. "You should be grateful that *he's* the one I'm in contact with."

"Why?"

"I'm told the first clone was less religious, so to speak. He wanted to kill you."

"Still why?"

Kinoshita shrugged. "I don't know. My guess is that he felt like a shadow, or a surrogate, and the only way he could feel like a true human being was to be the *only* Nighthawk."

"That doesn't make sense. I can see why the second clone feels the way he does, but even when I was a young man, I don't think I was as stupid as you make the first clone sound."

"That's why he died," answered Kinoshita promptly. "He *wasn't* you, not where it counted. He had your physical attributes, but not your memories or your experience. Truth to tell, I don't think he *wanted* to be the Widowmaker." He frowned. "I wish he had taken me with him on his assignment. I might have been able to help him."

"Well, you helped the second one."

Kinoshita snorted his disagreement. "He never needed my help. Or anyone else's, for that matter."

"He seems to have made quite an impression on you," noted Nighthawk.

"He was *you*," answered Kinoshita. "At the height of your powers. Before you decided you didn't especially want to be you any longer."

"I like being *me*. I'm Jefferson Nighthawk. I don't want to be the Widowmaker anymore."

"This is getting a little too schizophrenic for me," interjected Sarah. "I think it's time to start considering our options."

"It's too soon," replied Kinoshita. "It'll be another ten or twelve Standard hours before we can be sure no one's following us."

"That doesn't mean we can't *consider* what to do,"

insisted Sarah. "We should have some plan of action. Two plans, really—one if we're being followed, one if we're not."

"If we're being followed, the only course of action is to lose them," said Kinoshita. "We're not going to fight them, ship to ship or man to man."

"All right," said Sarah. "Then let's see what worlds are within reach, on the assumption that no one's coming after us."

Kinoshita brought up a holograph showing their sector of the Inner Frontier, and had the navigational computer highlight every oxygen world that had been colonized.

"Fare-Thee-Well, Giancola II, Chrysler IV, New Angola, Lower Volta, Rashomon, Purpleveldt, Tiger-stripe III, Nelson 23, Tallgrass . . ." Kinoshita's voice droned on and on, identifying each world.

"How about this one?" asked Sarah, pointing to a blue-and-green world about the size of Tumbleweed.

"Thaddeus," said Kinoshita.

"Thaddeus? That's a human name. Who was he?"

"I don't know. It could be the name of the navigator who first discovered the world, or the Pioneer who opened it up, or one of the planet's more famous citizens."

"It looks interesting."

"It looks like every other world," commented Nighthawk dryly.

"That's not so, Jefferson," she said. "Look at how much water it has. And cloud cover. Except for its size and location, it could be Earth itself."

"And except for my name, my looks, and my profession, I could be a chorus girl."

"All right, all right," she said. "Which world do you want to land on?"

"Makes no difference to me," answered Night-hawk. "Thaddeus is as good as any."

"Good." She turned to Kinoshita. "When you know for sure we're not being followed, divert to Thaddeus."

"All right," he said. "Let's get a readout and see what we can learn about it." He uttered a terse command to the computer, and instantly a series of notations appeared and hovered before their eyes:

Planet: Alpha Flint IV
Local Name: Thaddeus
Atmosphere: 19% oxygen, 78% nitrogen, 3% inert gases
Gravity: 98% Deluros VIII normal
Population: 18,203 humans, no indigenous sentient
*   species*
Currency: Maria Theresa dollars. Most locals will accept
*   Far London pounds or New Tanganyika shillings. The*
*   Oligarchy credit is not honored.*

"Is that okay with you?" asked Sarah.

"Yeah," said Nighthawk. "I've got enough Far London pounds to see us through until I convert my credits."

"I wonder why they don't accept them?" mused Kinoshita.

"The farther you get from the Oligarchy, the more certain the people are that it won't last any longer than the Republic or the Democracy did, and they don't want to be stuck with useless money."

"But that's silly!" protested Kinoshita. "The Republic and the Democracy each lasted for over two millennia, and their currency was always honored by their successors."

"Well, then," said Nighthawk, "just accept the fact that Frontier folk haven't got much use or faith in whoever's ruling the galaxy this month." He paused, blinking furiously, and turned to Sarah. "Give me another pill. Everyone's getting blurry again."

She did as he asked, and a moment later he was sleeping peacefully, while she sat down next to him, clasping his limp right hand in her own smaller ones.

It was ten hours later when he woke again, this time feeling physically healthy but starving. He and

Sarah vanished into the galley for half an hour, and when he reemerged, sated, Kinoshita announced that they had not been followed and were now approaching Thaddeus.

They landed within an hour, summoned a robotic cart, and had it unload their luggage.

"Where to?" asked Nighthawk.

"I must take your luggage through Customs," replied the robot. "If you'll head seventeen degrees to the northeast, you will come to the Immigration Station, where you will be processed. You can pick up your things once you have passed through."

"Thanks," said Nighthawk. They headed off in the direction the robot had indicated until they came to Immigration, a small, computerized station that was able to handle only one person at a time.

Nighthawk stepped forward.

"Name?" asked the computer.

"Jefferson Nighthawk."

"Occupation?"

"Retired."

"Purpose of visit?"

"Tourism."

"Thaddeus is an agricultural and mining world with no tourist industry."

"It's also possible that I might choose to become a permanent resident of Thaddeus."

"Alone, or with the other members of your party?"

"With my party."

"I must access your primary bank account to ascertain that you have sufficient funds so you will not become a burden to the Thaddeus economy."

"My primary account is on Deluros VIII, but it's in credits," answered Nighthawk. "I do have some accounts in Far London pounds, if you'd prefer."

"With your permission, I will access all of them."

"Fine."

The computer read the microscopic account

numbers on Nighthawk's passport, paused for some ten or twelve seconds, and then returned the passport.

"I am pleased to welcome you to Thaddeus."

"I'll need a map and a list of hotels, restaurants, and realtors."

"Processing your request . . . done." The map and lists suddenly appeared. "Here you are."

"Thanks."

Nighthawk walked through the station and waited for Sarah and Kinoshita to join him. They rented an airbus and drove it to the nearby town, then registered in the hotel—a room for Kinoshita, a suite for Nighthawk and Sarah.

"I should contact my son and tell him where I am," she remarked as they finished unpacking.

"Wait."

"Why?"

"Let's make sure we like it here first."

"All right—but we left Tumbleweed in such a hurry that I never told him we were going."

"He's half a galaxy away, and he contacts you about once every ten days—and only to ask for money. He can wait for a week or so."

She sighed. "I suppose so."

Nighthawk got to his feet. "I'd like a beer. You want to join me? I'll order from room service."

"I think I'd rather take a bath," she replied. "We were cooped up in that stuffy little ship for a long time."

He shrugged. "As you wish. I think I'll go down to the bar. I'll be back in time for dinner."

He left, took the airlift down to the main floor, and entered the hotel's bar, where he ordered a beer and took it over to an empty table. While he was wondering whether to call Kinoshita and treat him to a drink, a young man, dressed in brilliant colors, walked up.

"You're *him*, ain't you?" said the young man.

"I'm me," said Nighthawk.

"You can't fool me," said the young man. "I've

seen your holo a hundred times. You're older, but you're him. You're the Widowmaker."

"You want an autograph, right?" said Nighthawk sardonically.

"I want to be the man who killed the Widowmaker."

"You and ten thousand others," said Nighthawk. "Go home, son, while you still can."

"You're afraid to face me, right?"

"Okay, I'm afraid to face you. You made the Widowmaker back down. Now go away."

"Goddamn!" said the young man. "You really *are* afraid to face me, aren't you?"

"Right as rain, kid. Now leave me alone."

The young man was silent for a moment, lost in thought. Finally he spoke again: "No, I got to fight you. If I tell people you backed down, they'll never believe me. But if I kill you, they'll *have* to believe me."

"I'm not fighting anyone," said Nighthawk. "Beat it. Or sit down and I'll buy you a beer."

"Oh, you'll fight me, Widowmaker," said the young man confidently.

"You think so, do you?"

"I saw the woman you came in with. You'll fight me now, or you'll fight me after I kill her, but one way or the other you'll—"

He was dead, his forehead a bubbling, smoking goo, before he could get out the final words.

Nighthawk was on his feet instantly, looking around for other challengers. There were eight men and a woman in the bar. None seemed disposed to go for their weapons.

"He called me out," said Nighthawk. "I tried to send him on his way."

"We all heard, Widowmaker," replied the nearest man.

"You know who I am?"

"He wasn't exactly trying to keep it a secret." The man looked down at the corpse. "Still, that wasn't what I'd call self-defense. He never knew what hit him."

"That's what will happen to anyone who threatens the woman I travel with," said Nighthawk. "You might pass the word."

As he walked out the door and took the airlift back to his suite, he knew that word of the incident would spread, and from now on every young punk out to make a reputation would goad him into a fight by threatening Sarah.

Something had to be done—and by the time he got off the airlift, he knew what that something was.

Chapter 22

◆ ◆ ◆ ◆ ◆ ◆ ◆ ◆

◈

"*I want you to stay in the suite until word gets out that* I've left the planet," said Nighthawk. "Order your meals here. Don't go outside for any reason. Then, after a couple of days, pack up and book passage to Serengeti."

"The zoo world?"

"Right. Go to the western continent. There's only one lodge there, so you'll be easy for me to find." He frowned. "At least, there used to only be one lodge. It's been a long time since I was there." He paused. "Don't worry if I don't show up right away. It could be a couple of months."

"Where will you be in the meantime?"

"I have work to do."

"Why can't I come with you?"

"Don't make me answer that," said Nighthawk. "It'll just hurt your feelings."

"I want to know."

He looked into her eyes. "You'd be in the way."

"Oh, Jesus—who are you going to kill?"

"Just do what I ask, all right?"

She wasn't happy, but finally she stopped arguing and agreed.

Three men sat in a lobby at the Newton II spaceport. They all wore weapons, as almost everyone did on the Inner Frontier, but they were relaxed, drinks in hand, joking with one another.

Jefferson Nighthawk approached them from behind. None of the three paid him any attention. He pulled out his projectile pistol and swiftly and efficiently put a bullet into each of their heads.

A woman screamed. A number of people ducked or threw themselves to the floor. Two spaceport security men raced over, weapons in hand.

Nighthawk held up his passport and his ancient but still-valid license. "My name is Jefferson Nighthawk, and I'm a licensed bounty hunter. There was paper on these three men." He produced hard copies of the Wanted posters.

"Sonofabitch!" exclaimed one of the security men. "The Widowmaker—in *my* spaceport!"

The second security man checked the holographs against the dead men's faces and IDs.

"It's them, all right."

Nighthawk turned to the small man who was standing some fifty feet away.

"Get the body bags and put 'em on ice."

Kinoshita nodded and went about his work.

Her name was Jenny the Dart, and she was a freelance assassin whose weapon of choice was a tailor-made pistol that shot poison darts with deadly accuracy.

She was just emerging from a chic restaurant on Roosevelt III when she found herself facing Jefferson Nighthawk.

"Hello, Jenny," he said.

"Do I know you?" she asked.

"No reason why you should."

"What do you want with me?" she demanded.

"You've killed seventeen innocent men and women, Jenny," said Nighthawk.

"Innocent of *what*?" she said contemptuously.

"That's not for me to answer. You're worth two million credits dead or alive. The choice is yours."

She made the wrong choice, and fell lifeless to the pavement less than a second later.

"Ito! Take care of her."

He called himself Will Shakespeare, which was a pretty impressive name for a man who had never learned to read or write. But he knew that everyone respected Shakespeare, even though he'd been dead for more than six millennia, and he decided that they'd respect anyone who wore Shakespeare's name.

Of course, the fact that he'd killed more than fifty men and aliens didn't hurt, either.

He was after Number 51 when a tall, slender, gray-haired man blocked his way.

"Who the hell are you?" demanded Will.

"Francis Bacon," said Nighthawk.

"Step aside, old man."

"I'm afraid I can't do that. I'm pissed at you for stealing all my plays."

Will Shakespeare was still trying to figure out what Francis Bacon was talking about when the laser burned a smoking hole in his chest.

The last of them bore the simplest name and the biggest reward. It was an alien known simply as Bug, and it wore no weapons at all. Instead, it killed with the natural fluids of its body, spitting them as far as thirty feet with enormous force and accuracy, then watching as they instantly ate into flesh and bone until all was swiftly dissolved.

Nighthawk found Bug in the squalid Alien Quarter on Pretorius V, making its rounds of the quarter, exacting tribute from the other aliens for not killing them this month.

He approached Bug directly and silently, which had always worked up to this point, for the killers he approached had no reason to be apprehensive about his presence, and were totally secure in their gifts.

But Bug knew that Men didn't enter the Alien Quarter without a reason—and the only reason a Man would approach it was the four-million-credit reward. Bug waited until Nighthawk was twenty feet away, then ejected a stream of deadly spittle from its mouth. Nighthawk had been quicker in his youth, but he was still fast enough to throw himself to the ground beneath the alien's saliva, pulling out his Burner and firing it as he fell.

It was a fatal shot—but Bug's race possessed exceptional vitality, and even though it knew he would soon be dead, it still had enough strength to raise itself on what passed for its knees, face Nighthawk, and eject another lethal stream.

Nighthawk was ready, and turned it to steam even as it flew toward him, then burned out Bug's eyes, just in case it had the strength to spit once more before it died.

It was an intelligent maneuver, for Bug didn't collapse for another thirty seconds.

Nighthawk got to his feet and surveyed his surroundings. Dozens of aliens of all races were staring at him, but none was approaching.

"Ito! Get this garbage off the street."

They were eleven days out of Thaddeus, and were on their way to the Binder X bounty station to turn in the bodies and collect the rewards.

"Six bodies, fifteen million credits," intoned Kinoshita. "That's a *lot* of money."

"I *need* a lot of money."

"Now that you're the Widowmaker again, it seems to me that you can get money whenever you want it."

"How many times do I have to tell you that I'm not the Widowmaker?"

"After these last two weeks?" said Kinoshita. "One hell of a lot more times than you have, and then I still won't believe you."

"You're a fool."

If I'm a fool for thinking that the Widowmaker is back in business and has just killed six outlaws for the bounties, thought Kinoshita, *just what does that make* you?

Chapter 23

◆ ◆ ◆ ◆ ◆ ◆ ◆ ◆

"Okay, you've got your money," said Kinoshita as their ship reached light speed and left the Binder system far behind them. "What now?"

"Now I spend it."

Kinoshita blinked rapidly. "*All* of it?"

"That's right."

"You must be buying Sarah one hell of a present."

"A very ephemeral one," answered Nighthawk.

"So where are we going?"

"I know where *I'm* going. I don't know if you'll want to come along."

"I told you before," replied Kinoshita. "I go where the Widowmaker goes."

"And I told you: I'm not the Widowmaker."

"All right," said Kinoshita. "I go where *you* go. Do you like that better?"

"You may change your mind."

"Try me."

"I'm going to Deluros."

"Deluros?" repeated Kinoshita, surprised. "What the hell is there to do on Deluros?" He looked sharply at Nighthawk. "Are you going back to kill your lawyer?"

Nighthawk smiled. "You know, that's a tempting thought—but no."

"What then?"

"I can't tell you."

"Why the hell not?"

"Because you and I have always been lawmen, and I'm going to commit a felony—probably several of them. If I'm captured, I know I can't be broken. You're a good man, Ito, but I don't know that with the right combination of torture and drugs you won't talk." He paused. "And since I can't tell you my reasons for going to Deluros, I officially release you from whatever duty or fealty you feel you owe me."

"Do you want me to come or not?" asked Kinoshita bluntly.

"You can make my mission a little easier if you come with me, but I'll accomplish it regardless."

"Okay, I'm coming."

"You're sure you don't want to consider it?"

"I *did* consider it. I'm coming."

"Then, thank you."

"Everything we've done since we left Thaddeus was part of a plan, right?"

"That's right."

"You really plan to commit a felony?"

"At least one."

"I hope to hell you know what you're doing," said Kinoshita.

"That makes two of us," answered Nighthawk.

Chapter 24

♦ ♦ ♦ ♦ ♦ ♦ ♦

Deluros VIII was a freak.

It possessed ten times Earth's surface area, with an almost identical atmosphere and gravity, two large freshwater oceans, and enough landmass to house thirty-three billion bureaucrats in some semblance of comfort. It was right in the middle of the most populous, star-studded section of the galaxy, while Earth was isolated not even in the galactic suburbs, but out in the rural extremities of the Spiral Arm.

Man began moving his seat of government to Deluros VIII during the middle years of the Republic, and by the time of the Oligarchy, almost four millennia later, even huge, awesome Deluros VIII was inadequate to the task of ruling Man's empire.

There were fourteen other planets in the Deluros system. The outer six were all gas giants, totally useless for Man's purposes, but Deluros VIII provided the answer to the Oligarchy's problem. After consultation with hundreds of leading scientists, it was decided to break it apart with a number of carefully placed and extremely powerful explosive charges. The small fragments, as well as the larger irregular ones, were then totally obliterated. The remaining forty-eight planetoids were turned over to the largest governmental departments of the Oligarchy: one was reserved for Agriculture, one for Alien Affairs, one for Exobiology, and so on. (The military promptly claimed the four largest, and was soon feeling cramped for space.) Domes were erected on each planetoid, worldwide bureaucratic complexes were constructed, and life-support systems were implemented. The orbits of the planetoids were adjusted so that they danced their slow minuet around huge Deluros millions of miles from each other, and tens of thousands of ships sped daily between the enormous ruling world of the Oligarchy and its forty-eight extensions.

"You know," remarked Kinoshita, staring at the viewscreen as they approached their destination, "every time I see Deluros VIII I feel like some kind of country bumpkin. The last time I was stationed here they announced that you could finally reach any location on the planet without taking a step outside. Can you imagine that—a single building that covers the whole goddamned planet?"

"I seem to remember some parks, and some outdoor pavilions," said Nighthawk.

"Oh, I didn't mean to imply that every inch of the planet is a building. It's got courtyards and atriums—some of them extending for hundreds of acres. I'm just saying that you don't *have* to step outside to get from any point to any other point unless you want to—and sometimes not even if you want to."

"I suppose they think that's something to be proud of."

"They think it's an achievement unmatched in the history of architecture."

"Then they belong here," said Nighthawk, making no effort to hide his distaste.

"There are worse places to be," said Kinoshita. "It's got the best restaurants and theaters and art galleries and sports stadiums and hotels in the galaxy."

"No argument," replied Nighthawk. He studied the screen, which was showing a transmitted view of the world, as seen from a height of some forty miles. "It's got everything you could ever want—except character."

"You think those dry, dusty, underpopulated worlds we work on have character?"

"When you're standing on one of them, you know it's that world and not any other."

"You know it on Deluros, too," responded Kinoshita. "It's the only world where the buildings are so tall that there are only a few places where you can stand on the ground and still see the sky."

"And you think that's a good thing, do you?"

"I didn't say that. I said it makes Deluros as unique as any Frontier world."

"You can meet every man who lives on a Frontier world before you can find a given location on Deluros."

"That's because you're a stranger here. I've lived on Deluros VIII. It's the most logically laid-out city I've ever seen. What it lacks in character it makes up for in order."

"If you say so."

Nighthawk went to the galley for a beer. When he came back, they had entered an orbit some six hundred miles above the huge planet's surface. Once, centuries ago, there had been many spaceports on Deluros VIII, but after the increasing congestion caused numerous fatal crashes, the planetary planners gave in to the inevitable and created dozens (then hundreds, and still later thousands) of orbiting hangars. Ships docked at the hangars, Customs and Immigration were to be cleared hundreds of miles above the surface, and only authorized government-run shuttles were allowed to transfer the tens of millions of daily (and sometimes hourly) travelers to and from the planet.

The ship's radio suddenly came to life.

"Please identify yourself and your ship," said a cold, emotionless voice that might or might not have been human.

"My name is Jefferson Nighthawk, passport number M3625413C, fifteen days out of Alpha Flint IV on the Inner Frontier. My ship is a Class H 341 Golden Streak, registration number 677LR2439. Crew of two: myself and Ito Kinoshita."

"I have just uploaded a list of 174 contraband substances into your ship's computer. Are you carrying any of them?"

"I doubt it, but I won't know until I study the list."

"You have a Class H ship. *It* can answer." Pause. "In fact, it just has. You are cleared to dock at Hangar 113H. I will feed the coordinates and bay number to your navigational computer."

"Fine. Is that all?"

"Have you a place to stay? I can make reservations at more than six thousand hotels."

"I'd like a two-bedroom suite in the vicinity of the John Ramsey Memorial Medical Center. Price is no object."

"Done. You have a guaranteed suite at the Wellington Arms Hotel, a six-mile underground monorail ride from the John Ramsey Memorial Medical Center. Your confirmation number is 10733422. If you choose to cancel your reservation, you must inform the hotel by 1800 hours, Deluros North Central Time."

"Thank you."

"When you clear Customs and Immigration, take either a blue-coded or orange-coded shuttle, then transfer to a Sector 179 shuttle at the Ten-Mile Platform."

"Blue or orange?" repeated Nighthawk.

"That is correct. Any other shuttle will land you on the wrong platform, and you will be thousands of miles from your destination."

"Thank you."

"My deep scanner informs me that you are wearing the following weapons: a laser pistol, a sonic pistol, a projectile pistol, and two knives; and that Ito Kino-shita is wearing a laser pistol and a sonic pistol." The voice paused. "You will have to leave these aboard your ship, as weapons are not permitted on Deluros VIII."

"I'm a licensed bounty hunter," said Nighthawk. "Most planets have a provision that allows bounty hunters to carry registered weapons."

"Deluros VIII did indeed have such a provision," said the voice, "but it was repealed in 5073 G.E. You are not permitted to bring any weapons with you."

"All right. Is there anything else?"

"I have no further questions, though of course Immigration and Customs will have their own questions to ask you. Your ship will finish docking in approximately ninety seconds. I can answer any questions you may have during that time."

"None," said Nighthawk, breaking the connection. He looked at Kinoshita. "Can you say 'overregulated'?" he asked wryly.

"It may be overregulated, but there hasn't been an assassination on Deluros in almost two decades."

"What about simple everyday murders?"

"Most husbands and wives don't need guns to kill each other," replied Kinoshita with a smile.

"A point well taken," said Nighthawk.

There was a momentary silence. Then: "Why did you want your weapons?" asked Kinoshita.

"I feel comfortable with them."

"I wish you'd stop lying to me," said Kinoshita. "I'm here in your service. I'm prepared to lay down my life for you. I'll continue to do it whether you lie or not, but I'd feel less like a fool if you'd start telling me the truth."

"You'll know soon enough," said Nighthawk. "And I don't plan on firing any weapons."

"Then why do you think you need them?"

Nighthawk shrugged. "Things don't always go according to plan."

The ship shuddered as it docked in its bay, and a

moment later Nighthawk and Kinoshita were in one of many long lines at the Immigration center. The questions were more numerous and more thorough than on the Frontier worlds, but eventually they got through them, had temporary visas added to their passport cards, and accompanied their luggage through the Customs scanners.

Finally they went to the Deluros Departure Terminal, walked past some two dozen shuttles carrying the wrong color coding, finally found a blue-coded one, and boarded it along with almost a thousand other passengers. It took less than two minutes to fill to capacity, and then they were floating down to the enormous Ten-Mile Platform, which encircled the planet like a wedding ring. Here they took a seemingly endless tram ride until they came to a Sector 179 shuttle and boarded it.

It took this somewhat larger shuttle almost ten minutes to fill to capacity, and then it took off for the surface. They landed gently on a rooftop some two miles above the ground, took an airlift to the subbasement level, and found themselves in an enormous monorail station. Hundreds of tracks crossed the area, heading out in all directions, and as quickly as one train departed another instantly appeared to take its place.

"So how do we find the Wellington Arms?" muttered Nighthawk.

"We ask," said Kinoshita, walking to one of a hundred Tourist Aid computers along the wall.

"Good afternoon," said the computer as its lens registered his proximity. "How may I help you?"

"How do I get to the Wellington Arms from here?" asked Kinoshita.

"Take Monorail Number 206 South to Station RL—that will be four stops from here. Transfer to Monorail Number 1701 East, and exit at Station SC."

"And we're there?"

"You will be within walking distance," answered the computer. "Once you are at Station SC, ask another Tourist Aid computer for exact directions."

"Thanks," said Kinoshita. He turned to Nighthawk. "That's the way you do it around here. There are natives who still need these damned things to get around." He walked toward the platform for Monorail Number 206 South, and Nighthawk fell into step beside him. "I don't imagine things have changed all that much in a century. Don't you remember using the computers when you came here before?"

"I was ninety percent dead," answered Nighthawk. "I don't remember much of anything." He glanced around at the mass of humanity, each hurrying toward one of the six hundred monorails. "Just as well," he added. "If this is living, I think I'd prefer death." He looked around contemptuously. "Hell, I'd welcome it."

"You've been on the Frontier too long."

"And you haven't been there long enough," countered Nighthawk.

They soon reached the platform, caught a tram, and within a few minutes had transferred at Station RL, ridden another mile, and exited at Station SC.

This time it was Nighthawk who approached the computer to get directions to the hotel—"One block east of Exit 14, turn north 172 feet to the front door, enter, turn left 80 feet to the registration desk"—and in a few minutes they were finally in their suite.

A robot brought their luggage up to the room, explained how to use the plethora of gimmicks and gadgets that had been built into the suite, and then made a graceful retreat.

"Nice place," said Kinoshita, walking around the sitting room that connected the two large bedrooms. "I wonder how much it's costing you?"

"I'm sure they'll tell me before I leave."

"You ready to talk yet?"

"We've been talking all day."

"You know what I mean," said Kinoshita. "Why are we here? What is there on Deluros that managed to pull you halfway across the galaxy?"

"Nothing," said Nighthawk. "Yet."

"I don't understand."

"That's just as well."

"Damn it, Jefferson!"

Nighthawk walked to the door. "I'm going out for a while. Wait here for me. If I'm not back by morning, check to see if I'm being held in one of the local police stations, and if I am, bail me out."

"That's all?" said Kinoshita. "Can't I do anything more?"

"Yes, you can," replied Nighthawk. "I need a piece of information from you. Once you give it to me, you'll figure it all out or you're a lot dumber than I think you are."

Kinoshita stared curiously at him. "I know something of value to you?"

"It's nothing I can't find out for myself, but you can save me some time and give me some details I can't get anywhere else."

"If it's mine to give, you're welcome to it," said Kinoshita. "What is it?"

"An address."

Chapter 25

◆ ◆ ◆ ◆ ◆ ◆ ◆

◈

*Gilbert Egan rode the walkway down the long under-*ground corridor to his office, passing a pair of security checkpoints. He stood before his door, waited for the scanners to register his retina, weight, and bone structure, and entered.

The door slid shut behind him, and Egan walked over to his cluttered desk. He stopped, startled, when he saw the man sitting behind it.

"Good morning, Dr. Egan," said Nighthawk. "Pull up a chair. We've got some business to discuss."

"Who the hell are you?" demanded Egan.

"You really don't recognize me?"

"Should I?" asked Egan, staring at him. Then: "Shit! You're Nighthawk!"

"That's right."

"What are you doing here?" demanded Egan. "How did you get in?"

"I never saw a security system I couldn't crack," said Nighthawk.

"But you missed a century of technological improvement!" Egan pointed out.

"Yeah . . . but I'm the Widowmaker."

"You realize you've broken at least one law, sneaking in here, possibly several."

"Suppose you let me worry about that," said Nighthawk.

"Fine," said Egan, getting to his feet. "You can discuss it with the authorities." He walked to the door.

"Take one step outside or call for help and I'll break another law," said Nighthawk, and Egan turned to find himself covered by a Burner.

"How the hell did you get a gun on Deluros?" demanded Egan, half frightened, half outraged.

"I have my methods."

"What do you want?" asked Egan. "If it's money . . ."

"Shut up and listen," said Nighthawk. "All I want from you is a favor. As for money, I'm prepared to pay you ten million credits for it."

"Ten million credits?" repeated Egan unbelievingly. "Who do you want me to kill?"

"No one. In fact, quite the opposite."

"I don't know what you're talking about."

"There have been two clones of me already," said Nighthawk. "I want a third one."

"Your eplasia has been cured, and you seem to be in good health," said Egan. "Why do you want another clone?"

"My reasons are no concern of yours. I want it, and I'm prepared to pay handsomely for it."

"Creating a clone is a felony, punishable by—"

"Five million is for your skill," interrupted Nighthawk. "The other five million is for the risk."

"Look," said Egan, "even if I wanted to, you've got the wrong man. I'm just a doctor who specializes in cryonics."

"I'm offering to make you a filthy-rich doctor."

"Mr. Nighthawk, my job was keeping you alive. That's what I do. Others cloned you; I didn't."

"You know who they were." Nighthawk tossed a thick envelope on the desk. "There's ten million credits in there in unmarked bills. Talk one of them into it for two million and you've earned eight million credits for ten minutes' work."

"How long have I got to make up my mind?"

"About a minute," said Nighthawk. "If your answer is no, that's the end of it—with this stipulation: If you tell anyone I was here, I'll kill you. And believe me, I can do it before they can stop me."

"I believe you."

"Thirty seconds left."

"All right," said Egan. "I'll do it."

He reached for the envelope, but Nighthawk was faster, pulling it back. He opened it up, pulled out five million credits, and placed them on the desk.

"A down payment," he said. "You get the other half when I get the clone."

Chapter 26

* * * * * * * *

◈

It was an hour after midnight as Nighthawk approached
Egan's exclusive apartment, more than a mile above the
planet's surface.

Security was tight in the luxury titanium-and-
glass structure. He had to get a robotic doorman to an-
nounce his presence while still on the main floor. After
he was cleared, his ID and retina were read by the airlift
before it ascended, and when he got off at the 353rd
floor he went through the entire process again before
he was permitted to leave the vicinity of the lift.

There was a final scanning at Egan's front door,
and at last he was allowed to enter the apartment. A
sleek, shining robot butler greeted him and ushered
him into a huge, sprawling room with constantly changing murals on the walls. State-of-the-art furniture floated
gently a few inches above a plush carpet with an almost
hypnotically swirling pattern, and a huge window looked
down on a cloud layer.

Two men were waiting for him. Egan stepped forward to greet him.

"Jefferson Nighthawk, I'd like you to meet . . . ah . . . Doctor X." Egan gestured toward his companion. "Doctor X, Jefferson Nighthawk."

"I've worshiped you ever since I was a boy," said Doctor X, and as he extended his hand, Nighthawk saw that he was a rather pudgy man in his mid-forties. "I'm thrilled to meet you in the flesh. I was responsible for one of your clones—the one who met such an unfortunate end in the Solio system."

"Egan's explained the situation to you?"

"Yes."

"And you're willing?"

"That's why I'm here. I have only one stipulation: I would like your assurance that both you and the clone will be returning to the Inner Frontier, and will not attempt to reside in the Oligarchy. It could be most awkward if the authorities learned of this."

"You have my word."

There was an uneasy pause.

"Aren't you going to insist on knowing my real name?" asked Doctor X.

"Will knowing it make the operation go any smoother?" asked Nighthawk.

"No, of course not."

"Then why should I care?"

"Well, I thought—"

"The police can't extract what I don't know," explained Nighthawk. *And besides, Ito will be following you home later tonight, so if you do betray me, he'll know who to kill.*

"A very reasonable attitude," said Doctor X, looking much relieved. "When do you wish the process to begin?"

"What's wrong with tomorrow?"

Doctor X shook his head. "I can't be ready by then."

"Why not?" asked Nighthawk. "You're the cloning

expert. I assume you have access to everything you need."

"It's not that simple, Mr. Nighthawk," explained the medic. "When your first two clones were created, we had the protection of the most powerful law firm on Deluros VIII, so we didn't have to be quite so secretive. But for *this* procedure, security must be absolute, as we all face many years of imprisonment if we should be apprehended. I'll need at least three days to set up a lab, perhaps four. Then I'll be ready to take some skin scrapings from you."

"All right," said Nighthawk. "How many people will be involved in the project?"

"Four at most, all of them trusted aides of many years' standing—and all of them men and women who worked on your first clone."

"And how long will the whole process take?"

"The science of cloning has made phenomenal strides, despite government opposition," said Doctor X. "We can have a fully grown clone operational in six to eight weeks. The progress in nutrient solutions alone has been—"

"I don't care *how* it gets done," Nighthawk interrupted him. "Only *when*."

"I assume you care about more than that," responded Doctor X.

"For example?"

"For example, what physical age should the clone be?"

Nighthawk considered for a moment. "Twenty-five."

"If you wish, we can supply him with your memories, right up to the instant of his creation."

"What will that require?"

"Just you."

"Explain."

"The transfer of memories is rather like uploading data from one computer to another, but because the brain is so much more complex and subtle, it's a much longer process. I'd have to put you under for almost three days. There's some minimal danger involved in being anesthetized for so long, but you seem to be in fine physical condition. I think you can handle it."

"Out of the question."

"There's no other way. That's how your second clone received your memories. Of course, you were already unconscious; frozen, in fact."

"The answer is no."

"It won't hurt at all," Doctor X assured him.

"I'm not worried about a little pain," said Nighthawk. "But I'm commissioning a felony, and I've already made both of you wealthy men. There's no guarantee that you won't simply forget to wake me up."

"I assure you—"

"I'm sure you do," said Nighthawk, "but what are your assurances worth to a dead man?"

The doctor shrugged. "I don't know what I can say to convince you . . ."

"The only way I can be convinced is to have a confederate standing next to you with a gun—but that might make you nervous, and I don't want you doing the wrong thing at the wrong time." *Hell, in a way, it's just as well he won't have my memories. I don't want to be the Widowmaker anymore; he's got to revel in it.*

"All right," agreed the doctor with obvious reluctance. "We'll attach him to educator tapes day and night for the final month of his development. He'll enter the world with a basic education, fully able to speak, read, and write."

"That'll be good enough," said Nighthawk. "I'll handle it from there."

"We'll also have to give him a childhood," added Doctor X. "They'll be false memories, of course, but pleasant ones."

"No," said Nighthawk.

"I beg your pardon?"

"No memories are better than false ones."

"You're speaking from ignorance, Mr. Nighthawk," replied Doctor X. "If he enters the world as an adult with no memories at all, he'll soon be a basket case. As he develops his own very real memories and you educate him, the ones we give him will soon fade."

"You're sure?"

"We kept tabs on the first clone until he left on his mission—and by that time, only a month or two into his existence, he had already jettisoned most of his false memories."

"You mean, forgotten them?"

"In a way. Once your new clone knows his memories are false, he will—how can I explain it?—push them into the attics and basements of his mind, replacing them with experiences he has undergone, experiences he knows to be true."

"How can he do that?"

"When you see an exceptionally realistic holographic entertainment, or experience a vivid dream, you accept it as real while it's happening—but once it's over and you realize that it was merely an illusion of reality, you have no difficulty separating it from real experiences, have you? Your clone will do much the same thing."

"You'd better be right," said Nighthawk. "This clone is going to be under enough pressure from the real world. I don't want him hallucinating or going schizoid because he can't tell his real experiences from his false ones."

"It won't happen," said Doctor X firmly.

"It better not."

Doctor X stared at Nighthawk for a long moment. "May I ask exactly why you want me to create him?"

"You can ask."

"You can trust to my discretion, Mr. Nighthawk."

"I'm sure I can," replied Nighthawk. He smiled humorlessly. "And my clone can trust to mine."

Another awkward silence.

"If we have nothing further to say to each other, I think I shall take my leave of you," said Doctor X.

"We have one thing further to say, or rather, *you* have," said Nighthawk. "I want an address."

"Where we're creating the clone, you mean?"

"That's the only address that interests me," said Nighthawk.

"As soon as I know, I'll tell Gilbert, and he can tell you. But I warn you, Mr. Nighthawk—we must have complete secrecy. Knowing where the clone is being created does not mean you will be allowed access after the day we take the scrapings."

"Suppose you let *me* worry about that."

Egan was unable to suppress an amused chuckle.

Chapter 27

The handsome young man opened his eyes and tried to focus them.

"Where am I?" he rasped.

"Take it easy, son," said Doctor X. "You're just fine."

"Who are you?" Suddenly the young man looked very confused. "Who am *I*?"

"You're in a very private hospital," said Doctor X. "This gentleman standing next to me is Jefferson Nighthawk. He'll answer all your questions."

He nodded to Nighthawk, then left the room.

Nighthawk walked over to the bed. "How do you feel?"

"I don't know. Nothing hurts—but I can't remember how I got here."

"I'll be happy to tell you. But let's wait a few moments until you've got all your wits about you. You've been asleep a long time."

The young man stared at Nighthawk, puzzled. "Do I know you?"

"Not yet, but you will."

"What was your name again?"

"Jefferson Nighthawk."

The young man blinked furiously. "I seem to remember something about a Jefferson Nighthawk, something I heard or read when I was a kid. Were you an athlete or something?"

Nighthawk smiled. "Something."

"Wait a minute," said the young man, his face taut with concentration. "Now I remember! You're the Widowmaker!"

"That's right."

"But you've been dead for a century!"

"Not quite," replied Nighthawk. "I contracted an incurable disease, and I voluntarily submitted myself to cryonic freezing for a century—until it wasn't incurable any longer."

"Well, I'm thrilled to meet you," said the young man. "But what interest does a famous lawman like you have in someone like me?"

"More than you can imagine."

The young man looked expectantly at him.

"I don't like beating about the bush," continued Nighthawk, "and I don't think you do, either. So I'm going to tell you some things that are going to be difficult for you to accept. You won't believe them at first, but they're true nonetheless. Are you ready for them?"

The young man sat up, and just as quickly collapsed back onto the bed.

"Damn!" he muttered. "What's the matter with me?"

"Nothing."

"There's *something* wrong, maybe the same disease you had," he continued. "I can't even sit up by myself."

"You'll contract the disease eventually," said Nighthawk, not without sympathy, "but you don't have it now. You can sit up, and if you try a few more times, you'll do it without any problems." He paused. "You're not sick. You're just using muscles that you've never used before."

"What are you talking about?" said the young man. "All I'm doing is sitting up."

"Listen to me, son," said Nighthawk. "You haven't used *any* of your muscles. Ever."

The young man stared at him. "All right, who the hell are you really?"

"I told you: Jefferson Nighthawk."

"You also told me you're more than a century old, and that I've never used any of my muscles before. Why should I believe anything you say?"

"Only one reason," said Nighthawk. "I'm telling you the truth. I *am* Jefferson Nighthawk." He paused, staring at the young man. "And so are you."

"What asylum did you escape from?"

"Here," said Nighthawk, handing a small mirror to him. "Take a good, hard look."

The young man studied himself very carefully, occasionally glancing up at Nighthawk with a curious expression on his face. Finally he handed the mirror back.

"What am I—your son?"

"Not quite."

"I'm not in the mood for guessing games."

"You're my clone," said Nighthawk.

The young man grabbed the mirror back and studied it even more intently. Finally he shook his head vigorously. "You're crazy! I remember things, things from when I was a boy!"

"I know. Those are memories you've been allowed to borrow until you get some of your own."

"Bullshit! Nobody borrows memories!"

"You think not?" said Nighthawk. "You remember growing up on a farm on Pollux IV. You always wanted a dog, and finally your father imported one from Earth itself. You called him Snapper. He drowned when the two of you were swimming in the river together, and you blamed yourself for years. Your first love was Becky Raymond from the neighboring farm, but you never told her. When you were fourteen, you—"

"Enough!" shouted the young man. He stared at Nighthawk. "I never mentioned Becky to *anyone*, not even my brother!"

"I know."

The young man looked distressed. "*Was* there a Becky?"

"Yes," said Nighthawk, not without sympathy. "But not in your past. In someone else's."

The young man was silent for a very long moment. Finally he spoke: "I thought clones were illegal."

"They are."

"Then how—?"

"I paid a lot of people off."

"Why?"

"That's something we have to talk about. I think we'd better wait until you've assimilated what I've already told you. Tomorrow, perhaps."

"Now," said the young man firmly. "You've just told me that yesterday I was a blob of protoplasm, and today I'm a younger version of you. I want to know why."

"Good," said Nighthawk approvingly. "I don't like procrastination in my Jefferson Nighthawks."

"You make it sound like I'm not the only clone."

"You're the third—though you're the first I've laid eyes on."

"I take it the first two didn't make it out of the lab?" said the young man.

"They made it out," said Nighthawk. "The first one was killed. The second one's still out there somewhere, with a new name and a new face."

"Why do you need so many clones? In fact, why do you need any at all?"

"While I was frozen here on Deluros, inflation was

so rampant that I was in danger of running out of
money before they found a cure for my disease. Someone on the Frontier offered a lot of money for a clone
that could wipe out some enemies. That was the first
one. He did his job, but didn't outlive it. That bought
me a few years. The second clone bought me the rest of
the time I needed."

"And you're cured now?"

"That's right."

"So why am I here?"

"I need you for a totally different reason." Nighthawk smiled ruefully. "It seems that the galaxy needs a
Widowmaker more than this particular Widowmaker
needs the galaxy."

"I don't know what you're talking about."

"I'm an old man," said Nighthawk. "I've got a
woman I care for, I'm tired of killing, and I want to live
out the rest of my life in peace."

"So?"

"There are a couple of million men and women
out there who want the Widowmaker dead, enemies
the first two clones made, enemies I don't even recognize. I killed some of them in self-defense, but now
word is out that the Widowmaker is back on the Frontier, and every punk kid who's out to make a name for
himself is seeking me out." He paused. "Do you see
where this is leading?"

"Yeah," said the young man, staring at him curiously. "I think so."

"Well, let me eliminate any doubts right here and
now," said Nighthawk. "Son, I created you to take over
the family business."

Chapter 28

•   •   •   •   •   •   •   •

They had no trouble leaving the Deluros system. Nighthawk, with five million credits still in his possession, spent a million on the best fake fingerprints, retinagrams, and passport money could buy, and the scanners never once blinked as they passed the clone through.

It took them three days to reach Serengeti and pick up Sarah, who was less surprised than Nighthawk had expected, and then they went deep into the Inner Frontier, finally landing on Dustdevil, an arid little world circling an unimpressive binary.

Then Nighthawk began the task of training the new Widowmaker.

"Kinoshita will teach you everything you need to know about shooting and freehand fighting," said Nighthawk. "He did a fine job with the first clone, who was just about your age."

"Then why did the clone die?" asked the young man.

"Not for lack of physical abilities. You've got every one I ever possessed, and you're not even in your prime yet." Nighthawk paused. "The problem with the clone was that his head wasn't on right. Ito will train your body; I'll train your mind."

The young man flew through the air and landed heavily on his back.

"You cheated!" he said accusingly.

"Of course I cheated," said Kinoshita. "You think murderers and assassins don't cheat? Let's try it again."

"Give me a minute to catch my breath."

Kinoshita walked over. "Sure, kid. Take your time." Suddenly he kicked the young man full in the face.

"You son of a bitch!"

"First rule of the game, kid," said Kinoshita. "Never trust a killer."

"I'm surprised the first clone didn't kill you," muttered the young man, getting to his feet and facing his antagonist.

"He tried," said Kinoshita, dodging a heavy blow, grabbing an arm, and twisting suddenly. "But just like you, he telegraphed."

The young man went sprawling again.

"I thought you were going to—"

"Never picture what you think I might do, kid," said Kinoshita. "If you do, that's what you're subconsciously prepared for. And if I do anything else, it takes you a fraction of a second to adjust."

"I wonder if the pair of you aren't wasting your time," said the young man. "I don't think I'll ever be good enough to take you."

"Of course you will—and sooner than you think. After all, you're Jefferson Nighthawk."

"Okay," said the young man, getting back to his feet. "Let's try again."

A moment later he went flying again—but this time he was a fraction of an inch and a fraction of a second closer to landing a near-deadly blow on Kinoshita.

Every afternoon and every evening they would sit in the living room, man and clone, and the master would lecture the pupil.

"The thing to remember," said Nighthawk, "is that by the time there's paper on a man, he's no longer wanted on suspicion of anything. He's a killer, and while some of them are the nicest men and women you'd ever want to meet, the Widowmaker lives by a simple code: To feel compassion toward a killer is an insult to his victims."

"What if he begs for mercy?"

"You don't give him a chance to," responded Nighthawk. "This isn't some holo drama where two gunmen face each other on the street. You're the good guy; always remember that. The law's on your side. And being the good guy gives you certain advantages. You know what your enemy looks like; he doesn't know who you are. You know his history; he doesn't know yours. You can study him at your leisure; he can't study you. And when you're ready to take him, you don't have to call him out and give him a chance to blow you away. If he's sitting at a bar or a card table or a restaurant, you walk up behind him and put a bullet or a beam in his ear."

"Women, too?"

"You think a woman with a Burner or a Screecher can't kill you just as dead as a man can?"

"I was raised not to—"

"When a woman takes a shot at you, you'd better overcome your feelings—or you're dead."

"Okay, there are four targets at three hundred yards," said Kinoshita. "Blow 'em away."

The young man drew his Burner and fired it, hitting three and missing one.

"Not bad. Not good, but not bad."

"Why is this important? Who am I going to shoot from this far away?"

"Hopefully no one."

"Then why—"

"You can't always get in close to the man you're after. Sometimes it's a matter of taking him out from a quarter mile away or letting him escape."

"All right. Let me try again."

This time he hit all four.

"Not bad."

"Damned good, if you ask me," said the young man.

"I didn't ask you." Kinoshita held up a stopwatch. "You hit four targets in three seconds. If those were men, the last two had time to blow you away. Let's cut that time in half."

"Then what?"

"Then you do it with the other hand. And with every other weapon we've got around here. And then you do it at four hundred yards, and at five hundred."

"Five hundred? It can't be done.

"Sure it can. That old man in the house can still do it, and you're going to be better than he ever was."

"Do you really think so?"

Kinoshita smiled. "Kid, training Widowmakers is one of the very best things I do."

After a month, Nighthawk said good-bye to Sarah and Kinoshita and took the clone to Barrios II, home of the Gomorrah Palace, the biggest whorehouse on the Inner Frontier.

Nighthawk picked up the tab as the young man went to bed with a different woman every morning and evening for five days.

"Aren't you interested in sampling their wares at

all?" asked the young man as he emerged from yet another bedroom.

"I've got what I want waiting for me back on Dustdevil." He paused. "I think it's about time we were getting back there."

"Well, I want to thank you for bringing me here."

"No need to thank me. It's part of your education."

"It is?"

Nighthawk nodded. "The first clone died because he let his hormones rule his mind, and it impaired his judgment. He fell for the first woman he saw, and eventually she proved his undoing. I don't want that happening to you."

The young man frowned. "And what I've been doing this past week will prevent it?"

"It's probably not in the textbooks, but yeah, it will."

"How?"

"By showing you that sex is enjoyable no matter who you have it with, and that all women are pretty much the same between their legs—just like all men. It's what's between their ears that makes you decide whether or not to slay a dragon for them."

"You've got an interesting way of making your point."

"I know what would impress me," said Nighthawk, "so I know what will leave a lasting impression on you."

And, of course, it did.

While Kinoshita spent the next sixty days honing the young man's marksmanship and fighting abilities, Nighthawk took over at nights, lecturing on strategy, preparing him for the thousand situations he might confront. Then one day he pulled out a nondescript bottle of whiskey and poured each of them a glass.

"I don't like it," said the young man, making a face. "It burns my throat as it goes down."

"You don't have to like it," said Nighthawk. "You just have to learn to hold it, to drink and not let it affect your judgment or your abilities."

"Why?"

"Because a lot of information you need will be obtained in taverns, and if you're not used to drinking, it could have a very adverse effect on your reactions."

"You're sure I have to do this?"

"Trust me, you'll learn to enjoy this before long." Nighthawk paused. "Once I know you can handle your liquor, we'll start on a couple of very mild drugs that you'll use in situations where you've got to visit drug dens. You'll enjoy them, too, but don't forget that the object of the exercise is to build up a resistance to them."

"How will you know when I've built up enough resistance?"

"When you can drink a pint of booze, outscore me at the shooting range, and then beat the crap out of Kinoshita."

"You really think I'll be able to do all that?" asked the young man dubiously.

"Sooner than you think," promised Nighthawk.

And finally the young man was as ready as Nighthawk and Kinoshita could make him.

"That's it," said Nighthawk. "I've taught you everything I can. Today you are the Widowmaker."

"It's awkward to be called nothing but Kid or Son or even Widowmaker. I need a name."

"That seems fair enough. What name do you like?"

"Considering my pedigree, yours—now that I'll be leaving soon and it won't cause any confusion."

"Then you can have it," said Nighthawk.

"What name will *you* take?"

"I've got a name. I've had it for a century and a half, and I'm not about to change it." Nighthawk paused. "Tell you what: For the very brief amount of time we're still together, you can be Jeff and I'll be Jefferson, just so we'll know who Ito and Sarah are speaking to."

"Sounds good to me."

"Fine. Now let's grab some dinner, and get a good night's sleep. You've got a big day ahead of you tomorrow."

"I do?"

"Yeah," said Nighthawk. "We're going to find out just how good a teacher I am."

"Great!" said Jeff, unable to hide his enthusiasm. "What are we doing?"

"We're going to a little world called Tumbleweed."

Chapter 29

◆ ◆ ◆ ◆ ◆ ◆ ◆ ◆

❖

Nighthawk walked into the tavern, looked around at the empty tables, then walked over to the bar and ordered a beer.

"A word of advice," said the bartender. "Take your beer and leave."

"Oh?"

"Those two guys who ran you out of here are still on the planet. Somebody's got to have spotted you, and they'll know about it soon, if they don't already."

"Thanks for the tip."

"A lot of people blame you for cutting and running back when they showed up," said the bartender. "Not me. They didn't see what those two guys could do; *I* did." He paused. "I don't think you could have taken them both even when you were a young man, no matter what everyone says about you. Besides, Tumbleweed never did anything for you; I don't figure you owe us anything. I mean, hell, you already killed that whole gang of drug runners out at the spaceport. Everyone knew they'd be there, but only you went out to face them. I figure *we* owe *you*."

"I appreciate that," said Nighthawk. He picked up the beer and walked to a table.

"Then appreciate a little friendly advice and get the hell out of here while you still can."

"Not today."

"They'll be here any minute," said the bartender. "Take my word for it."

"I'm sure they'll be here," replied Nighthawk. "But they don't want me."

The bartender shrugged. "Well, I did my best." He went back to polishing glasses and sorting oddly shaped bottles of alien liquor.

Nighthawk slowly sipped at the beer. When he'd finished half the glass, Mr. Dark, dressed in an elegantly tailored dark gray outfit and shining boots, entered the tavern. He was followed a moment later by Mr. Night, clad in a severely cut black outfit with matching boots and holster.

"Well, look who's come back to visit us, Mr. Night," said Mr. Dark, staring at Nighthawk.

"I think he was very rude to leave so suddenly the last time we met," said Mr. Night. "You hurt my feelings, Mr. Nighthawk."

"You have feelings?" asked Nighthawk.

"There!" said Mr. Night in mock distress. "See? You did it again!"

"Still," said Mr. Dark, "we're very glad you came back, whatever your reasons."

"Are you really?"

"Certainly," said Mr. Dark, withdrawing a colorful silk handkerchief and dusting an invisible speck from his tunic. "We have some unfinished business, if you'll recall."

"And this time," added Mr. Night, "I don't think we'll let you leave the tavern until we conclude it."

"I have no business with you," said Nighthawk.

"Ah, dear me," said Mr. Dark, "the poor man's memory has left him. I suppose that happens when you reach a certain age."

"True," agreed Mr. Night. "We'd almost be doing him a service, putting him out of his misery now that his mind has ceased to function properly. He'd probably thank us if he understood the true nature of our actions."

"You talk too much," said Nighthawk, taking another swallow of his beer.

"Bold words for an old man who's about to die, Widowmaker," said Mr. Dark.

"Wrong on both counts," said Nighthawk.

The two men stared at him curiously.

"Would you care to explain yourself?" said Mr. Night.

"First, I'm not about to die, and second, I'm not the Widowmaker."

"What new foolishness is this?" demanded Mr. Dark. "You're Jefferson Nighthawk, aren't you?"

"Yeah, that's right."

"Then you're the Widowmaker."

Nighthawk smiled and shook his head. "Not anymore. In fact, he's standing right behind you."

They turned to find themselves facing the clone, who stood in the doorway.

"Gentlemen," continued Nighthawk, "say hello to the new Widowmaker."

"What are you talking about?" said Mr. Night suspiciously.

"We had a drawing, and he won."

"He looks a lot like you," said Mr. Dark.

"Good genes."

"Son? Grandson? Nephew?"

"Yes," answered Nighthawk. "And that's all I've got to say to you." He gestured to the young man. "From this point on, talk to *him*."

"But talk quickly," added Jeff. "My lunch is getting

cold, and all I really want to do is kill you and get back to it."

"He *talks* like a Widowmaker, Mr. Dark," said Mr. Night. "What do you think?"

"I think he's trying to frighten us, Mr. Night," said Mr. Dark.

"Is it working?" asked Mr. Night.

"Not that I notice," said Mr. Dark, turning to face the young man. "What's your name, substitute Widowmaker?"

"Destiny," said the young man.

"I beg your pardon?"

"Fate. Death. Take your choice."

"Pretty damned silly names, if you ask me."

"I didn't. But if you don't like them, I'm also Jefferson Nighthawk."

"You borrowed the name as well as the title?"

"I inherited it."

"Poor boy," said Mr. Night. "You're about to inherit what we had planned for *him*."

"And you're about to inherit two plots in the local cemetery," answered Jeff. "I reserved them this morning, once I knew you were still on the planet."

"You sound pretty confident when we're standing side by side," said Mr. Dark. He began edging away from his partner. "Are you just as confident when we stand apart?"

"It just means you won't hit each other when you fall."

You're talking too much, enjoying it too much. Don't wait for them. Just pull your guns and blow them away. They're talking for a reason; start paying attention to what they're saying and you're a dead man.

"Well, that's very considerate of you, isn't it, Mr. Night?" said Mr. Dark.

"Absolutely," agreed Mr. Night. "In fact, I don't know when I've met a more considerate doomed man."

As Mr. Night spoke, Mr. Dark went for his weapon.

Jeff drew his guns faster than Nighthawk's eye could follow. Before Mr. Dark's gun could even clear its holster, he and his partner were both dead, each with a smoking black hole placed directly between their eyes. Mr. Night got off a single wild shot as he fell across a table; it hit a century-old bottle of Cygnian cognac, spraying the kneeling bartender with broken glass and wildly expensive liquor.

Nighthawk got up, walked over, and stared at the corpses, then looked at Jeff.

"How did I do?" asked the clone.

"Goddamn!" exclaimed Nighthawk. "I was as good as the legends say!"

"Better, even," offered Jeff.

"I thought you were going to get yourself killed with all that talking."

"Oh, that," said Jeff with a shrug. "I was just waiting for one of them to go for his weapon."

"Why?" asked Nighthawk. "I've told you over and over that it's not a sporting contest. You don't have to be a gentleman about it."

"I knew I could take them," answered Jeff calmly. "I just wanted to see how good they were."

"You'd never seen them in action before. How could you know you'd take them?"

"I'm the Widowmaker."

There was a long, thoughtful pause.

"Yeah," agreed Nighthawk. "I guess now you are."

Chapter 30

♦   ♦   ♦   ♦   ♦   ♦   ♦   ♦

❖

The new Widowmaker loved his work. He loved the competition, the fame, the adulation, even the notoriety. As word spread across the Frontier worlds that he was back in business, he liked the fact that people whispered and pointed as he walked past. He liked the service he got in hotels and restaurants and taverns, he liked the willingness of the women he met and the subservience of the men.

His career had begun on Tumbleweed, but he remained there only a few hours.

He tracked down three murderers on Giancola II and killed them all.

He killed four more on Greenveldt, even though they were lying in wait for him.

Backbreaker Kimani called him out on New Angola, and though Kimani was seven feet tall, four hundred pounds of rock-hard muscle, and a former freehand heavyweight champion, the young Widow-maker killed him in hand-to-hand combat.

By the time he reached Chrysler IV, his reputation had preceded him. The entire Wilconi Gang was waiting for him, all twelve of them. Nighthawk offered to lend a hand, but Jeff rejected the offer, walked into an obvious death trap, and killed them all, suffering only a single flesh wound in his left leg.

He followed Lady Platinum to her hideout on Fare-Thee-Well, took her prisoner as she tried to seduce him, and broke both her arm and her jaw when she pulled a hidden knife on him.

His final test came on Lower Volta. Nighthawk didn't even know he was going there, and would have advised him to at least take Kinoshita along. But he went in alone, against the rest of the drug runners that Nighthawk had killed months earlier on Tumbleweed, and picked them off one by one until all forty were dead.

"I couldn't have done better myself," admitted Nighthawk when Jeff returned to their home base on Dustdevil and told him of his exploits on Lower Volta.

"I *am* yourself," replied Jeff with a smile.

"Yes, you are," said Nighthawk. "Sometimes I forget."

"You must have loved your life before you came down with eplasia," said Jeff enthusiastically.

"I don't know that I ever thought about it. I had a job, and I did the best I could at it."

"Now there are three of us abroad in the galaxy—you, me, and the second clone. Do you know what we could accomplish if we joined forces?"

"I don't know the other clone's name or how to contact him," said Nighthawk. "Besides, he doesn't want anything to do with me—or, by extension, you." He paused. "And I created you so that I could finally retire and be left alone."

"I know," he said wistfully. "Still, it would have been fun."

Nighthawk smiled. "I trained you just right, and I made you the right age."

"What do you mean?"

"I mean I haven't thought of my work as *fun* since I was twenty-five."

"How could you not enjoy it?" replied Jeff. "People know me everywhere I go." He grinned. "And you can't beat the pay."

"The pay is commensurate with the risk."

"Hell, even the risk is exciting."

"Well, you didn't inherit my outlook, that's for goddamned sure," said Nighthawk. "I was right not to give you my mind. You might as well enjoy yourself for as long as you can."

"With your skills, I just might live forever," said the young man.

"I approve," said Nighthawk. "That's the only way for a man in your profession to feel. If you ever start thinking that Death happens to you instead of to other people, it's time to hang it up." He paused. "We haven't discussed it, but someday, in a year or a decade, you're going to wake up and think you're developing a rash over your whole body. You'll wonder what you ate, or rubbed against, and when you can't come up with an answer, you'll wonder exactly what was in the atmosphere of the last world you visited. And the whole time you're wondering, the rash will get worse, and soon you'll understand that it's not a rash after all. Your skin will literally start rotting away, and you'll realize that the problem isn't external, but internal, that you have eplasia."

"Maybe I won't get it."

"You're a genetic duplicate of me, which means you've got my weakness for it programmed into you. You'll get it, all right. The good news is that it's finally curable. All I want to tell you is to not wait until you're sure that's what it is. The moment you see a rash, get to a doctor—quick. If it's actually a rash and nothing worse, you haven't lost anything. But if he says it's eplasia, go to the best clinic you can find, and have them treat you immediately."

"I'll go to the one that cured you."

Nighthawk shook his head. "That's on Deluros, and we can't know that Egan and his friend have kept their silence. You're illegal, remember?" Nighthawk paused in thought. "No, go to a world named Safe Harbor. I've never been there, but I'm told that they've got a hell of a medical facility—and that they have no use for the Oligarchy. If they find out you're a clone, they'll probably work all the harder to keep you alive."

"How come you didn't use it?" asked Jeff.

"There was no cure back then. I had to go to Deluros VIII to get frozen and wait for a cure."

"Okay, I'll watch for it. Just a simple rash, right?"

"Right."

Nighthawk leaned back comfortably on his chair. "Okay, it's finally done."

"What is?"

"Your education. That was the last thing I had to tell you."

"I'll be leaving in the morning," said Jeff. "Will you and Sarah and Ito be staying here after I leave?"

"I don't think so," said Nighthawk. "It's really not much of a world. I think we'll try settling on Tallgrass. They say it's a lot prettier."

"I'll check in with you from time to time."

"Please do. I'd like to keep up with who I've killed recently."

Chapter 31

• • • • • • • •

Tallgrass was pretty and green and temperate, with a pair of Tradertowns, a handful of farms, one large gold mine, and not much else. They bought a small home a few miles out from the larger Tradertown.

Nighthawk and Sarah spent a month remodeling it and putting it in order, while Kinoshita traveled to Nelson 23 with the clone, who captured three of the four Jimana Sisters, while killing the fourth.

"You know," said Sarah when they had finished working on the house, "I think I'm going to like this world even better than Tumbleweed."

"You're supposed to," replied Nighthawk. "That's why we moved here."

"You know what it doesn't have?" she continued. "A restaurant."

"You don't have to work," said Nighthawk. "I've still got a couple of million credits left, and nothing to spend it on."

"Look," she said, "you spent your whole life hunting down killers and rapists and the like, and now you want to rest. That's fine. But I *enjoy* working, and I'm good at what I do."

"I didn't say you couldn't work," replied Nighthawk quickly. "I said you didn't have to. I don't own you; you're free to do whatever you want to do. If you want to start a restaurant, start one. I'll be your best customer."

"Good. There's an empty storefront in town. I want to take a look at it. If there's room in the back for a kitchen, it's just about the right size."

"All right," said Nighthawk. "Let's go take a look at it."

They drove down the winding dirt road to the Tradertown and parked in front of the empty building.

"The realtor gave me the entry code," said Sarah, walking up to the door and uttering a seven-digit number. The door irised, and the two of them walked into the storefront.

"It looks smaller than the one you had on Tumbleweed," remarked Nighthawk.

"It is," she replied. "But I had an oversized kitchen there. I can accomplish the same here with half the space. Then, if we break through this wall"—she indicated the wall in question—"we could have, let me see, oh, probably six tables for two, four or five for four, and one for six. And of course we could push them together for larger parties." She began walking around the empty room. "Let's see. We'll need public rest rooms, and they'll take up some space, and—"

A single shot rang out, and the plate-glass front window shattered.

Nighthawk raced across the room and unceremoniously threw Sarah to the floor as a laser beam burned a hole in the wall directly behind where she had been standing.

"What's happening?" she asked, confused.

"Quiet!" he whispered. "And don't move."

Ten more bullets ripped into the walls, and a pair of laser beams began sweeping the room at waist height.

"Who is it?" demanded Sarah. "Nobody here knows us. There must be some mistake!"

"People don't shoot at me by mistake," muttered Nighthawk, slithering across the glass-covered floor on his stomach.

He raised his head a few inches, then ducked as one of the lasers sought him out.

"Come on out, Widowmaker!" yelled a voice. "We know you're in there!"

"Sarah, can you get to the back door?"

She nodded.

"Do it," instructed Nighthawk. "But don't go out, just in case there are more of them waiting back there for us. Let me know when you've made it and I'll join you."

Sarah crawled to the rear entrance, and Nighthawk got there a moment later.

"What now?"

"We're dead meat if we stay here," he said. "Those lasers will have the place in flames in another minute." He pulled out his own Burner. "I'm going out first. If you don't hear my gun hum, count to five and come out after me."

"And if I *do* hear shooting?"

He withdrew his Screecher and handed it to her. "Then do the best you can." He paused. "I don't think they're back there, though, or there'd have been gunfire from that direction, too. If no one's waiting for us out back, hide in the first building you come to."

"What are *you* going to do?"

"What I thought I was all through doing," he said bitterly.

He edged out the back door, Burner in hand. She waited, didn't hear the hum of Burners firing, and followed him. No one shot at her, and she headed off to her right, while he began moving left in a crouching trot, keeping to the shadows of buildings wherever he could.

When he'd gone to the end of the block, he sneaked a look back and saw that the building was indeed in flames. Three men were standing in the street in front of it, two armed with Burners, one with a bullet gun, obviously waiting for him to come running out of the smoking storefront.

Nighthawk edged around the corner. He was perhaps forty yards from them now, and they still hadn't seen him. He saw frenzied activity at the far end of the Tradertown, some three blocks away, and knew he'd have to move quickly before the firefighters ran head-first into the three would-be killers.

Nighthawk fired his Burner, and one of the three men dropped to the ground. The other two turned to face him, and he fired again. The man with the bullet gun spun around, his gun flying into the burning building, then fell to his knees, blood gushing out of his midsection.

The third man hastily fired at Nighthawk and missed. Nighthawk burned his gun hand away, then melted his burner where it lay on the street before he could reach it with his remaining hand.

"Who are you?" demanded Nighthawk coldly. "What do you want from me?"

"We came to kill you, you bastard!" grated the man with one hand.

"You made a mistake," said Nighthawk coldly. "I'm not the Widowmaker. He's off hunting scum like you."

"Fuck him!" spat the man. "You're the one who killed our brother on Bolingbroke!"

"Bolingbroke?" repeated Nighthawk. "That's what this is about?"

"We know you've come back from wherever you were hiding all those years. You've killed people all over the Frontier, and now you think you can hide from us by letting some other guy call himself the Widowmaker! Well, it's not going to work! You're a dead man!"

The man reached into a pocket for a tiny pistol, and Nighthawk fired and killed him before he could bring it into play.

The man who had been kneeling suddenly fell over on his side, also dead.

"Shit!" muttered Nighthawk. "I created a Widowmaker, gave him my genes and my skill and my name, and sent him out to take my place." He stared disgustedly at the three corpses. "This wasn't supposed to happen!"

Chapter 32

◆ ● ◆ ● ◆ ● ◆ ● ◆

◆

Nighthawk sat in a bar on Keepsake, a grubby little Frontier world. He'd been there for two hours, silent, sullen, unwilling to speak to any of the men and women around him.

As he was downing yet another drink, there was a commotion at the doorway.

"He killed Red Devil Korbite!" exclaimed one of the men.

"I'm buying for the house," said a familiar voice. "To law and order—may it always be shorthanded and in need of bounty hunters!"

Nighthawk looked up. "I was in need of a bounty hunter last week," he said, slurring his words slightly. "Where the hell were you?"

Jeff entered the tavern and approached Nighthawk. "What are you doing here?"

"Waiting for you. I heard Korbite was on Keepsake."

"He was. I'll buy you a drink to celebrate his timely demise."

"I don't give a shit what you're celebrating," said Nighthawk. "Sarah was almost killed last week."

Jeff's demeanor was instantly serious. "She was? Is she all right?"

"She's all right."

"Who did it? I'll take care of—"

"I already took care of them," said Nighthawk.

"Good. Then it's over."

"It's not over," said Nighthawk bitterly. "It's never over. I created you, and they're *still* coming after me."

"I thought you said they were after her."

"She was with me," said Nighthawk. "Not the safest place to be these days."

"I'm sorry to hear about it," said Jeff, "but what do you expect me to do?"

"I want you back on—" Nighthawk stopped, suddenly aware of the crowd. "I want you back on my new world, and I want you to stay there until I know no one else is looking for me."

"Don't be ridiculous. That could take years!"

"You're a young man. You've got years to spare."

"I've got more important things to do."

"I *created* you!" snapped Nighthawk. "I'm your goddamned god! What's more important than protecting me?"

"How many men have you killed since they woke you up?" shot back Jeff. "You can protect yourself."

"I don't *have* to protect myself. That's what you're for!"

"I'm not a fucking puppet!" yelled Jeff. "I'm my own man. You don't pull my strings!"

"Listen, kid," said Nighthawk, "I created you, and I can *un*create you."

Jeff laughed contemptuously. "Are you threatening me, old man?"

"You bet your ass I'm threatening you. I'm not

going to have Sarah killed, or be assassinated myself, because you're too busy chasing glory and big rewards. Everything you are you owe to me. That ought to be worth a little loyalty."

Suddenly the young man stared sharply at Nighthawk. "How long have you been drinking?"

"None of your business."

"I thought you could hold your liquor," said Jeff. "I guess I was wrong. You're not making any sense."

"You think it makes sense to turn your back on Sarah and me when I tell you we need you?"

"Look," said Jeff soothingly. "We can work this out. You're drunk now, and not thinking clearly. You can sleep it off in my ship, and we'll talk in the morning."

"I don't want your ship or your sympathy!" said Nighthawk. "I just want you to remember who put you here and who you owe for it!"

"I'm sorry you got old, and I'm sorry you've made enemies—but they go with the territory. There'll be people wanting to kill Jefferson Nighthawk as long as Jefferson Nighthawk's alive. Why don't you take a new name and maybe get a new face? It wouldn't be the first time someone's done that," he added meaningfully.

"I've spent enough of my time in hospitals. I just want to spend the rest of it in peace."

"Then go where they can't find you," Jeff shot back. "But don't drag *me* into it. You created me for a purpose, and I'm fulfilling it."

"The hell you are."

"I'm here to bring in the worst of the bad guys, the ones no one else can take—not to protect a broken-down old man whose past is starting to catch up with him."

"So that's what you think I am—a broken-down old man?"

"Look, I'm sorry I said it, okay?" said Jeff. "Just back off and calm down."

"This is a broken-down old man who taught you everything you know, and can still take you in a fair fight."

"Fine," said Jeff. "You can take me. Now try to calm down."

"Don't you give me orders!" bellowed Nighthawk. Before Jeff could react, he reached out and landed a heavy right to the young man's jaw.

Jeff fell to the floor, rolled once, and came up with guns in both hands. He found himself looking down the barrel of Nighthawk's Burner.

"Put 'em back where you got 'em," said Nighthawk. "*Very* slowly."

Jeff did as he was ordered.

"If you want to pull 'em out again, just say the word and we'll step out into the street."

"I don't want to kill you," said the young man. "You're like a father to me. *More* than a father."

"Funny," said Nighthawk. "You don't feel like a son to me."

"I'm sorry about that."

"You come back with me or you're going to be a lot sorrier."

"What the hell," said Jeff. "If it means that much to you . . ."

"It does."

"Then I'll come." He extended his hand. "Friends again?"

"Why not?" agreed Nighthawk, taking the young man's hand.

Jeff instantly pulled, twisted, and threw all his weight behind it. Nighthawk flew through the air and landed heavily on his back. He tried to reach for his Burner, but Jeff was too quick for him, and planted his foot on the older man's right hand.

"You're drunk," said Jeff, pointing a Screecher at him. "That's the only reason I'm letting you live." He squatted down and removed Nighthawk's Burner. "I know you always keep a knife in each boot. Reach for either of them and I'll blow both of your legs away."

Nighthawk glared at him, but said nothing.

"All right," continued Jeff. "Now I want you to

listen very carefully to me, old man, because I'm only going to say this once. I'm the Widowmaker. If you ever try to give me orders again, I'll kill you. If you try to publicly humiliate me again the way you did today, I'll kill you. If you follow me, I'll kill you. Do you understand?"

Nighthawk still made no reply.

"I'm leaving now," said Jeff. "I'm going out after Consuela Blood, and if you're here when I get back, I'll kill you."

He stepped away, tucked Nighthawk's Burner into his belt, and backed toward the door as Nighthawk slowly got to his feet.

"You're going to regret that," said the older man.

"Just remember what I said," replied Jeff. "If you're still here, I'll kill you."

"I'll be waiting," promised Nighthawk.

Chapter 33

♦ ♦ ♦ ♦ ♦ ♦ ♦

◈

The clone returned to Keepsake nine days later, with Con-
suela Blood's preserved body in his cargo hold. Even
before he left the landing field—no one would dignify
the little strip of barren ground by calling it a spaceport—
he noticed the crowd.

"What's going on?" he asked one of the bystanders
who lined his way to the tavern.

"Everyone's here to see the shoot-out."

"What shoot-out?"

"You and the old man," replied another member
of the crowd.

"Nighthawk?" replied Jeff. "He's sobered up and
gone home by now."

"The hell he has. He's waiting for you, just like he
said he would."

"That's suicidal," said Jeff, never slowing his pace
as he approached the tavern. "I'm everything he used to
be. He hasn't got a chance."

"He thinks he has."

"He was drunk. Once his brain starts working, he'll realize that there's only one way it could end."

"I'm telling you, he's waiting for you."

"How could he be that—?"

The young man broke off in midsentence as Nighthawk stepped out into the street.

"Why aren't you home with Sarah?"

"I've got business here," said Nighthawk.

"Have you been drinking again?"

"Not a drop."

Jeff frowned. "You remember what I said I'd do if you were still here?"

"I remember," said Nighthawk.

"It doesn't have to be like this. I still owe you something. You can leave right now, and I won't stop you."

"The Widowmaker doesn't cut and run from anyone."

"You're not the Widowmaker anymore," said Jeff. "*I* am."

"I say the survivor is," said Nighthawk, crouching as he pulled out his Burner.

He was fast, almost as fast as he'd been a century ago—but the clone was faster. Jeff fired his Screecher once, and Nighthawk literally flew back through the air, landed with a thud, and lay still.

Jeff walked over and looked down at the old man. Blood gushed out of his nostrils and ears, and his face was already discolored where dozens of tiny veins had burst under the onslaught of solid sound.

Finally Jeff looked up at the crowd.

"You all saw it," he said. "He went for his weapon first. It was self-defense."

"More than that," mused an elderly bystander. "It was inevitable."

Chapter 34

◆ ◆ ◆ ◆ ◆ ◆ ◆

Sarah and Kinoshita picked up the body and took it back to Tallgrass for burial. And when they brought it home, instead of taking it to the cemetery where the headstone was already planted, they laid it on its bed and kept watch over it.

Finally, after two days, an eyelid flickered.

"Where am I?" whispered Nighthawk.

"You're home," said Sarah.

"I can't hear you."

"You're home!" Sarah half-shouted.

"God, I feel awful."

"You *should* feel awful," said Kinoshita, raising his voice. "You were nailed by a Screecher at near-fatal force."

"Anything less and someone might have seen through it." Nighthawk winced. "My head's killing me. Give me something for the pain."

"I already have," said Sarah. "It should subside in a

few minutes. But you'll be in pain on and off for the next few weeks. Nobody's ever had a concussion quite like yours." She paused. "I think your hearing's pretty much gone. We'll have to see a doctor to enhance it."

"Old guys are allowed to be hard of hearing," said Nighthawk. He tried to smile, but the effort brought on another paroxysm of pain, and he lost consciousness.

When he awoke two hours later, Sarah and Kinoshita were still by his bedside, and the pain had subsided somewhat.

"Did it work?"

"Looks like it," replied Kinoshita. "Giving it a nine-day buildup was a good idea; an awful lot of people showed up to see you get killed. There are reports of your death all over the subspace radio bands."

"Good," said Nighthawk. "Then I can finally live the life I want to live, and *he* can live the life *he* wants." He reached out and clasped Sarah's hand in his own. "I just wish there'd been a better way to arrange it."

"It's over now," she said.

"Yeah, I think it probably is," agreed Nighthawk.

"Are you going to stay on Tallgrass?" asked Kinoshita.

"No. They found me here once already. I think we'll leave the Inner Frontier altogether, maybe go settle in the Spiral Arm where no one has ever seen me before."

"I wish you well," said Kinoshita. He stood up and walked to the door.

"You're coming with us, aren't you?" asked Sarah.

"I can't," said Kinoshita.

"Why not?"

"I'm a Samurai, like my ancestors."

"What's a Samurai?" asked Sarah.

"A warrior who serves his feudal lord," replied Kinoshita. "One whose life and death is at the disposal of his master."

"This is your master right here!" insisted Sarah, indicating Nighthawk.

"Not anymore," interjected Nighthawk weakly. He looked at Kinoshita. "It's time to leave. We both know that your duty lies elsewhere."

"Where?" demanded Sarah.

"He's waiting for me, somewhere out there beyond Keepsake," said Kinoshita.

"Serve him well," said Nighthawk. "He doesn't know it, but he needs you. He's got a lot more to learn."

Kinoshita turned to the man on the bed. "It's been an honor to know you." He shifted his feet awkwardly. "I wish I could stay . . ."

"I know," said Nighthawk.

"But you are merely Jefferson Nighthawk," he said as he opened the door. "And I serve the Widowmaker."

ABOUT THE AUTHOR

◆ ◆ ◆

MIKE RESNICK is one of the major names in science fiction, both as a writer and as an editor. He is the author of almost forty novels, eight collections, and more than one hundred stories and has edited twenty-five anthologies. He has been nominated for seventeen Hugos and eight Nebulas since 1989 and has won three Hugos and a Nebula, as well as scores of lesser awards. Among his best-known works are *Santiago*, *Ivory*, *Soothsayer*, *Paradise*, and the Kirinyaga stories, which have become the most honored story cycle in science fiction history. He lives with his wife, Carol, in Cincinnati, Ohio.

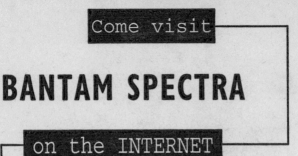